They were similar in height, their shoulders broad, their backs straight. No doubt about it: Matt was the best looking. He was blessed with the Irish charm. And she'd been crazy about the man since high school.

She took another picture and he looked toward her and winked. She felt the blush clear down her body. Oh, boy. She was in trouble.

"They sure make a heart-stopping sight, don't they?"

Alisa turned around to see Jenny, and close behind her was Jade.

"They're cowboys," was all Alisa would admit to.

Dear Reader

This is my fourth story in the series *A Quilt Shop in Kerry Springs*, and it's one that needed to be told.

Matt Rafferty wasn't planned to be one of my heroes, but after his appearances in the other books he earned his own story.

Eighteen months ago Matt returned home after the army, and he's had trouble adjusting to civilian life. He's also run into an old love, Alisa Merrick, and regrets how he ended it with her before leaving for overseas. This daughter of a US Senator isn't interested in his excuses.

It isn't until Matt and Alisa are stranded in a deserted building during a tornado, and become co-foster parents to a nine-year-old boy, that they discover there's still something between them.

They hit several roadblocks along the way. Alisa's political aspirations to follow her father start with her running for the town council. Matt has emotional scars from the war and is trying to start up a new business: Rafferty's Place. But when they're thrown together their feelings are too strong to resist.

I've loved spending time in this small Texas town. I hope you have, too.

Patricia Thayer

ONCE A COWBOY...

BY
PATRICIA THAYER

First published in Great Britain 2012
by Mills & Boon, an imprint of Harlequin (UK) Limited.
Harlequin (UK) Limited, Eton House, 18-24 Paradise Road,
Richmond, Surrey TW9 1SR

© Patricia Wright 2012

ISBN: 978 0 263

Harlequin (UK) p   papers that are atural, renewable
and recyclable pro   of sustainable
forests. The loggin and manufacturing proces onform to the
legal environmenta   gulations of the country   origin.

Printed and bound in Great Britain
by CPI Antony Rowe, Chippenham, Wiltshire

Originally born and raised in Muncie, Indiana, **Patricia Thayer** is the second of eight children. She attended Ball State University, and soon afterwards headed West. Over the years she's made frequent visits back to the Midwest, trying to keep up with her growing family.

Patricia has called Orange County, California, home for many years. She not only enjoys the warm climate, but also the company and support of other published authors in the local writers' organisation. For the past eighteen years she has had the unwavering support and encouragement of her critique group. It's a sisterhood like no other.

When she's not working on a story, you might find her travelling the United States and Europe, taking in the scenery and doing story research while thoroughly enjoying herself, accompanied by Steve, her husband for over thirty-five years. Together they have three grown sons and four grandsons. As she calls them: her own true-life heroes. On rare days off from writing you might catch her at Disneyland, spoiling those grandkids rotten! She also volunteers for the Grandparent Autism Network.

Patricia has written for over twenty years, and has authored over thirty-six books for Silhouette and Mills & Boon®. She has been nominated for both the National Readers' Choice Award and the prestigious RITA®. Her book NOTHING SHORT OF A MIRACLE won an *RT Book Reviews* Reviewers' Choice award.

A long-time member of Romance Writers of America, she has served as President and held many other board positions for her local chapter in Orange County. She's a firm believer in giving back.

Check her website at www.patriciathayer.com for upcoming books.

Books by Patricia Thayer:

DADDY BY CHRISTMAS
THE COWBOY'S ADOPTED DAUGHTER
THE LIONHEARTED COWBOY RETURNS

To the men and woman of our Armed Forces
who suffer from PTSD. Your wounds may be invisible,
but the pain is just as real.

CHAPTER ONE

SHE was late…again.

Alisa Merrick pressed down on the gas pedal of her silver convertible and the engine roared, then shot off down the county road. No way would she make the meeting on time unless she grew wings and could fly. And she needed the endorsement of the Kerry Springs downtown merchants to get elected to the council. She glanced at the dashboard clock and groaned.

That was when she remembered the shortcut. Okay, it was private property, but she knew the owners. The Raffertys were her neighbors. Surely they wouldn't care? Then Matt Rafferty came to mind. Maybe one would.

Alisa didn't have time to think just react so she took the sharp turn off the highway. Dust went flying as she made it onto the dirt road and started along the tree-lined road. Correction, overgrown trees and mesquite bushes made it difficult to see much ahead of her.

It didn't take long to realize this was a bad idea, and she needed to find somewhere to turn around and head back to the highway. Her vehicle couldn't handle this terrain. She didn't need to tear up the undercarriage of her car, but she had to keep going, hoping she made it out of this maze. Finally the trees thinned and she came into a clearing. That was when she saw the horse and rider. Too late.

Alisa hit the breaks and swerved to miss them. The huge rust-hued animal reared up and the rider went flying backward.

When she got the car stopped, she climbed out. "Oh, God. Oh, God," she chanted as she hurried to the down rider. The animal stood guard over the man who was facedown on the ground.

"Come on, boy. You need to move." She shooed him away, then knelt down beside the man.

Trembling, she felt for a pulse and thank God, she got one. With his hat gone, she recognized Matt Rafferty right away.

"Come on, Matt, wake up," she pleaded, trying to stay calm. "Matt, please.

He groaned and rolled to his side. He blinked and opened his eyes. She saw the dazed look. "Matt, are you okay?"

He groaned again. He was hurt. She touched him, and that was when he pulled away.

"Matt, it's me, Alisa. Please, please be okay."

Matt Rafferty fought to breathe. He tried to focus, but he felt himself slipping to that place he didn't want to go. Suddenly there was that familiar sound of the chopper blades, cutting through the clear sky. Help was coming. Was it enough? Would it be in time?

Somewhere in the background he heard a voice. A woman's soft, husky voice. Who was she? What was she doing here? He raised his eyes and slowly she was there.

"What the hell? Take cover," he shouted the order, but she didn't move. "Dammit!" He yanked her down beside him and pulled her close to him. "You're not a target."

"Matt!" she called his name.

He froze as the familiar voice broke through all the blurred sounds in his head. Then he felt her touch. He looked down at the woman next to him.

"Alisa…"

She smiled hesitantly, and his entire body reacted to it. As the fog began to clear, he wanted to run but he was weak as a kitten. Dammit. Not now. And not her.

She was the last person he wanted to see when he was like this. He glanced past her and spotted the car, recalling the noise that spooked his horse. He cocked his head as he caught the fading sound of the private helicopter that had sent him into a tailspin.

"Are you all right?" she asked.

"I'd be better if there weren't so much noise disturbing my herd, or my peace."

"Sorry, that was Dad's helicopter."

"Maybe he could take a different route," he grumbled as he rolled away, feeling the pain in his shoulder. He managed to sit up. "What are you doing here?"

She did, too. "Would you believe I was driving by?"

"Well, maybe you should keep driving. It's safer for all of us."

"I can't leave you," she argued. "You took a header off your horse."

He wanted to stand, but wasn't sure he could. "Well, I'm okay now, so you can go."

She shook her head and stood up. Brushing off her skirt, she said, "You need help, Matt. I'm calling 911."

"No! I'm fine."

She frowned. "You don't look fine. You're pale and you fell hard on your shoulder." When he didn't answer, she went on. "You might have dislocated it. And what on earth happened to you when the chopper flew over? You seemed really panicked."

He wasn't discussing this with her. "I'm more concerned that someone was trying to run me down." With every bit of strength he had left, he got to his knees, then after a slow shallow breath he stood up. It took a moment for the pain to subside, then he looked toward the tree to see his horse.

"Nick." He managed a low whistle, but it was loud enough to bring his mount to his side. He grabbed his hat off the ground and set it on his head. He could do this. He'd already revealed too much of his weakness. He didn't want her to see him like this.

Alisa stepped in front of his path. "You're not climbing back on that horse, Matt Rafferty."

She only stood about five-three. Even with her high heels she barely made it to his chin.

"Who's going to stop me?" he challenged.

When he started by her, she grabbed hold of his upper arm. He winced. "See, you're hurt."

"I can manage. I've taken spills off horses since I was a kid." He didn't need her hanging around here. That was when he saw the silver sport car. "What are you doing on Rafferty land, anyway?"

"I was taking a shortcut. I was late for a meeting."

"And that makes harming what or whoever gets in your path okay, does it?"

She jammed her hands on her hips. "I wasn't trying to harm anyone. I didn't see you."

Alisa Merrick was a gorgeous woman. A man had to be blind not to be attracted to that all long raven hair and those velvet-brown eyes. Her Spanish heritage showed in her defined cheekbones and rich olive skin.

And talking of skin, that was exactly what she did, got under his skin.

"Then you shouldn't have been racing around on private property."

"I told you I have an important meeting in town."

"What? Breakfast with your friends?"

"No, but if you must know—"

He raised a hand. "I don't want to know." His shoulder was throbbing. "I need to check my horse."

Matt eyed the dark chestnut stallion. A beautiful quarter horse, sixteen hands high and smart. He'd trained the champion himself. Matt ran a hand over his flanks, speaking softly, grateful he was okay.

He jammed his booted foot in the stirrup, but that was as far as he got when he reached for the saddle horn and pain shot through his shoulder. He cursed and stepped back.

"That's it." Alisa marched back to the car and grabbed her cell phone off the passenger seat. "You won't let me help then I'm calling someone who will."

Dammit. "Just hold on a minute."

When she looked at him, he felt his gut knot up just like it had three years ago. Right after he'd made love to her, then told her goodbye.

"You'll let me take you to the hospital?" she asked.

He finally nodded.

Alisa gave a sigh of relief but as she looked over the ruggedly handsome cowboy, she realized he could still cause her heart to race, and palms to sweat. She hated that. Matt Rafferty was last man she needed in her life right now. Who was she kidding? He didn't want her three years ago and he couldn't wait to get rid of her now. Well, she didn't want him, either. Just as soon as she got him to the hospital, she'd be gone, again.

"Let me call someone to get Nick." He unbuttoned his shirt pocket and pulled out his phone. He punched in the number to the barn.

When his foreman answered, he said, "Hey, Pete, I need a favor. I'm out by Old Mill Road about a half mile from the highway. Could you come and get Nick?"

"Is there a problem?" Pete asked.

Matt glanced at Alisa. "No, nothing I can't handle," he lied, knowing Alisa Merrick had distracted him once, and he couldn't let her do it again.

An hour later at the E.R., Alisa sat in the waiting room. She'd made several calls. The first to her father to cancel the meeting. This wasn't how she wanted to start her Monday. This wasn't how she wanted to start any day.

Alisa closed her eyes. Matt could have been seriously hurt because of her. Both her father and her brother Sloan had warned her so many times to slow down. She'd received two speeding tickets in the past year as it was, not to mention the times she gotten off with a warning because of the Merrick name. There had been times she enjoyed being a senator's daughter. But today, she'd caused an accident. Worse, she caused an injury. She still prayed it was minor. Whatever, Matt was in pain and it was her fault. No matter what a jerk he'd been three years ago, she never wanted to cause him harm.

She hadn't seen Matt much since his return home from the army, but seeing the incident today, she realized he hadn't come back unscathed. The man could argue all he wanted, but she knew he'd had a flashback. Not uncommon for men and women who had served in a war zone. Matt had done a tour of duty overseas and came home a hero. But at what cost?

The automatic doors opened and she looked up to see an older gentleman come rushing in, Sean Rafferty. Right behind Matt's father was his brother, Evan. Since she'd made the call, Sean came to her.

There was concern on his face. "How is he, lass?"

"When I dropped him off, he was complaining to the nurse."

Evan grinned. "That's a good sign. I'll go check on him."

They watched as Evan went to the nurses' station, then she turned back to Matt's dad. "I'm so sorry, Sean, if I hadn't taken the shortcut through your property…I truly didn't see Matt until it was too late."

The big Irishman took her hand. "We know you didn't mean any harm, Alisa. You have my permission to use that road anytime."

"Well, it was my fault, so I made arrangements to take care of Matt's medical bills."

"Let's not worry about that now."

"But he couldn't even get on his horse. So how can he work?" She knew that he was in partnership with his father and brother on the Triple R Ranch. Matt ran the cattle operation.

"There are enough ranch hands to handle the work," Sean assured her. "Although his injures might hold up the remodel at the bar."

"The bar?"

"That's right, you've been out of town awhile. We've recently purchased Rory's Bar and Grill."

"Mom said something about Rory retiring. So you bought the place." She smiled. "That makes sense since you've worked there for years. And you're famous bar-becue was born there. Will you continue to work there?"

Sean was a handsome man with thick white hair

and an Irish brogue. He'd recently married Beth Staley. "Sorry, I've retired from bartending. I want time with my bride, and together we'll promote Rafferty's Barbecue Sauce. So Evan and I are silent partners. The bar is Matt's baby. Of course, my barbecue will be on the menu along with the Rafferty Legacy wines."

Alisa was happy for them. "Seems while I was gone, I missed all the good stuff."

"Well, seems you've been busy, too," he said. "I've been hearing good things about you."

Since her parents were close friends of Beth and Sean, she knew immediately what he was talking about. "I only made it official just recently."

"Well, if my opinion matters, I think you'd be wonderful on the town council," Sean encouraged. "We need more young people running things around here. Your Da is so proud."

She'd always been a daddy's girl, even when they butted heads. She had some progressive ideas for this town. "Some people don't want change. That means I need to do some fundraising. I'm challenging an established town council member in Gladys Peters." Alisa had to prove to this district that she was worth taking a chance on.

"This town needs to be shaken up a little, and you're just the person who could do that." Sean's blue eyes lit up. "I have an idea. In a few weeks we're having a grand opening at the bar. Why not do a fundraiser there, too?"

Oh, no! She doubted Matt would be happy about this. "I'm honored, Sean, that you'd even consider it, but you're trying to get this business off the ground, I'm not sure that it's a good idea."

"What's not a good idea?

They turned around to see the Rafferty brothers. Both were tall and broad shouldered. Pure Texas Cowboys. Matt was the one wearing a sling.

"How are you feeling, son?" Sean asked.

"A little sore." He looked at Alisa. "There was no need for you to hang around."

Matt caught the hurt look on her face and regretted his words.

"I was telling your dad that I want to pay for your medical bills."

He didn't want any help from this woman, except to be left alone. "The insurance took care of everything. My shoulder was dislocated. So the doctor popped it back into place."

Alisa frowned, knowing that there had been so much more going on out there. Matt's reaction to the sound of the helicopter. She hated to think she'd triggered something. "Good. I'm glad, it could have been much worse." She locked her gaze on Matt, connecting with those mesmerizing, Irish-blue eyes. Suddenly everyone around them disappeared.

"Yeah, the doctor checked me out and said I was fine. The only thing is I can't lift anything heavy for a few days." He looked at Alisa. "So you're off the hook."

An hour later Alisa walked into the Blind Stitch Quilt Shop. On most days, this was where she'd find her mother. As an avid quilter, Louisa Merrick spent a lot of time with her group of friends in the Quilter's Corner. They'd work on projects together, like wedding and baby quilts. They'd do some for the craft fair in the summer and give the money to charity.

Alisa waved at Jenny Rafferty who was behind the counter, busy helping a customer. Her friend managed the store, and taught quilting classes. She was married to the sweet Rafferty brother, Evan. They had two adorable children, Gracie and Mick. There was a lot of reason to envy Jenny, but Alisa liked her too much to let that become an issue.

Alisa walked through the tables loaded down with swatches of colorful fabric, and the rows of shelves with sewing notions. Anything a quilter could ever need. She came to a wide doorway that led to the storefront next door where they held the classes. In the front of the room there was a large round table and around it sat a group of women.

There was Millie Roberts who also worked part-time at the store, Beth Staley-Rafferty, Sean's new bride, and her mother, Louisa Merrick.

She walked up to the group. "Hi, Mom," she said cheerfully to the nearly sixty-year-old woman.

Louisa wore her dark hair in a blunt cut that fell just below her ears. Her eyes were a deep brown. Some said the only difference between mother and daughter was their age.

"Good you're here," Louisa said. "I've been trying to call you. What happened this morning? Your dad said you had to cancel the meeting. Beth said you took Matt to the E.R."

She groaned. Of course the entire town knew. She nodded. "Sorry, Mom, that's why I didn't call." She looked at Beth. "I take it Sean filled you in?"

"Yes, he said Matt took a spill off his horse, but everything if okay."

Everyone looked at her for more information. "It was my fault. I was cutting through the back road at the Triple R. I must have spooked his horse, because the animal reared back and threw him off. I'm glad he's okay."

"Don't blame yourself," Beth told her. "That stallion is pretty high-strung as it is. No one can ride him except Matt."

"Well, I don't think he will be riding anything for a while."

"That might not be a bad thing." Beth said. "Matt's been working on the ranch during the day, and at the bar afternoons and evenings. He wants it opened as soon as possible."

Three years ago she'd gotten her chance to be with Matt Rafferty. He'd set down the rules, a no-strings-attached relationship for the weekend. But given the fact she'd been in love with him since high school, she'd jumped at the opportunity. Their forty-eight hours together had been incredible. Although she fell even deeper in love with Matt, he found it easy to walk out when she was still asleep, only leaving her a note.

It hurt that she didn't mean enough to him to wake her and say goodbye.

Matt had planned to make the army a career, so she'd been surprised when he'd come back to town eighteen months ago a civilian. Still there hadn't been a problem since she worked in Austin. He'd contacted her once, but she refused his calls, leaving him a not-too-nice message that she didn't want to see him again. She was probably one of the few women who had turned him down.

Then she'd returned to Kerry Springs to take a job on the Vista Verde housing project. Still Matt spent his time out on his ranch. And her main focus was on her job and budding political career. She didn't need complications.

"I should talk to Dad," she said to her mother.

"Good idea. Maybe you can reschedule the meeting with the merchants."

"I'm going to try to stop by and talk to each one individually." She said her goodbyes and headed out the door. It was a nice day and she decided to walk to her dad's office. Since he was retired now, he'd let her have some space for her campaign.

She crossed Main Street and smiled seeing the businesses that filled the old-fashioned storefront shops. Right here were the prime spots, Sayers Hardware Store, Shaffer's Ice Cream Parlor, just a block and a half down from the Blind Stitch Quilt Shop. She slowed on the sidewalk seeing old Rory's Bar and Grill. Okay, so it was nice to know that another business was coming in. Matt's new venture. Now that he'd be in town instead of the ranch, more than likely she'd be seeing a lot of him.

She shook off the thought of having her ex-lover around. More than that, she hated to admit that he still got to her. She spotted a familiar dark pickup parked at the curb. Matt was there...working?

She paused at the front door, then stepped inside, immediately seeing the disarray. There were stacks of wood piled all around and sawdust covered the old hardwood floors. The walls had been redone with bead board paneling stained a light natural color. All the window trims and baseboards were finished in a darker shade. The long oak bar had been sanded down and the old red vinyl booths were gone.

She heard a saw and followed the sound toward the back to a small alcove past the makeshift dance floor. That was where she found Matt. He was bent over a table saw, a pair of safety glasses protecting his eyes, a tool belt draped low on those slim hips. Her heart rate sped up.

Great! Another sexy image of this cowboy. Suddenly she knew this wasn't where she needed to be. She started to back away, so as not to disturb him. Engrossed in his work, he wouldn't even know that she was there. No such luck, she backed into a stack of wood that began to fall as she managed to catch her balance. Matt jerked around as he stopped the saw.

Glaring at her, he walked over. "I guess you didn't do enough damage this morning. Did you come back to finish the job?"

CHAPTER TWO

ALISA hadn't run from anything since Cody Grayson made fun of her in second grade, but she had to fight the urge and stand her ground with Matt.

"I take it you're still angry about earlier."

He raised his safety glasses to the top of his head. "Is that why you're here? You want to make sure I'm not going to press charges?"

She refused to let this man get to her. So far she hadn't had any luck with that. "No, I'm here because I'm concerned about you." She couldn't get rid of that protective feeling seeing him zone out this morning. "Are you going to deny that you were having a pretty intense flashback when I found you?"

"I don't have to deny anything. The doc gave me a clean bill of health." He cocked an eyebrow. "Of course if you want to practice a little nursing on me, I wouldn't turn it down." It was hard, but she ignored him. None of this was her business anyway.

"By the looks of things, you're not taking the doctor's advice anyway. You weren't supposed to work for a while."

"I'm not supposed to lift anything heavy." He nodded to the thin strip of wood. "I'm finishing up some trim work. I can handle that." He folded his arms. He'd taken off his collared shirt, revealing a fitted black T-shirt over his well toned chest and broad shoulders.

Oh, man. She tried to take a breath, but found it a struggle to draw air into her lungs. "I should let you get back to work then."

He smiled at her.

She hated that know-it-all grin of his. "What?"

"You've talked to me more today than since I've been home. Does that mean you've finally forgiven me?"

She didn't want to get into their brief past. "We haven't exactly had chances to run into each other. I've been busy working, and it looks like you have, too. Besides, you were the one who took off." Darn. She hadn't wanted to say that.

Those baby blues locked onto hers. "I tried to explain when I first returned home, but you weren't exactly eager to listen."

And she didn't believe his flimsy excuse then or now. She raised a hand. "Look, Matt, there isn't any reason to rehash all this. We've both moved on with our lives."

He nodded. "So…you're going to be a member of the town council. I better clean up my act, or you might shut me down before I open the doors to Rafferty's Place."

"Rafferty's Place." She liked that name. "Why would you think I'd want to shut you down? You're going to bring business to the downtown area. Besides, I haven't been elected, yet."

"A mere formality. Can't imagine a Merrick losing an election, not in Texas, anyway."

"I'm not my father." She didn't mean to reveal her insecurities. "I'm new at this."

"You're a natural, Alisa. People like you."

"Even you?" She about died on the spot. Why had she said that?

There was that grin again. "I've always liked you, but I refused to lead you on. I was committed to the army."

And the fact that he'd broken her heart had been his last concern at the time. She forced a smile. Being much older and wiser now, she refused to let him hurt her again. "What happened between us was a long time ago."

"So it's time to get over it," he finished for her as he started to walk toward her. "Can you, Alisa? Can you forget how good it was between us?"

She refused to back away. "Seems to me, I've been doing a pretty good job."

Matt knew he was playing with fire when it came to Alisa Merrick. Truth was, she had drawn him like no other woman he'd ever met. In other words, she was dangerous.

He bit down hard on the inside of his mouth as he eyed her in her slim skirt and high heels. But damn, if she didn't have one fine pair of legs. He turned his attention back to her face and tried to regain his composure.

"I'm glad, since I'm going to be a fixture on Main Street," he told her. "We'll be seeing each other a lot more. I'm hoping you'll come into the bar."

She glanced around. "That's right. I never congratulated you on your new venture. I can see already how nice everything looks." She smiled. "A lot of good things have been happening to the Raffertys. Your family members are quite the entrepreneurs."

He nodded. "Maybe one day we'll be up there with the Merricks."

She flashed a hurt look and he regretted his words.

"The Merricks are no better than anyone else in this town. Have any of us ever made you feel that way?"

He shrugged, trying not to let her see how she affected him. "Hey, you know me. Do I care what people think?"

Those ebony eyes stared up at him and he was about to confess how much she'd gotten to him. How much she still got to him.

"Seems as if you're changing, whether you planned to or not. From soldier to cowboy to businessman."

He didn't like that she saw through his act. "Yeah, we're both going places. But make no mistake. I'll still be that dust-eatin' cowboy."

Alisa straightened. "It looks like we'll both be busy the next few months, me with the election, you with the restaurant, and the ranch."

He nodded. "I'm putting in a lot of time here, and I've got roundup coming at the ranch. Not much time to party even if I wanted to."

"Doesn't sound like the Matt Rafferty I remember."

He had a lot of plans no one knew about. "I want to concentrate on making a future for myself."

"Well, I wish you luck."

"I appreciate that. You, too."

She glanced away. "I should let you go back to work." She pointed toward the door. "I need to get to my meeting."

"Drive safely," he told her. "I'll be inside and out of your way."

Her eyes rounded. "Not funny, Rafferty, not funny."

It was crazy, but he wanted to stop Alisa from leaving. Instead he tossed her a little attitude with a grin as she walked out the door, admiring the gentle sway of her hips.

He puffed out a breath, ignoring his body's reaction. "She's still way out of your league, cowboy. Just like Jody was. One a tough lesson, one I don't want to repeat. Sometimes you just got to pull it back, and take your losses." He only wished those words would stop the ache he felt in the middle of his chest whenever he saw her again. And by the looks of it, that was going to be a lot more often these days.

"Alisa?"

Alisa glanced up at her father. He sat on the edge of the desk in campaign headquarters. "Sorry, Dad. What did you say?"

"You were lucky this morning that no one was hurt."

At sixty, Clay Merrick was a handsome man. His looks and charm got him votes from women, and his ranching background helped with the male constituents. Truth was everyone liked him. He was a doting husband to Louisa, they'd been married close to thirty years, a family man without a hint of scandal. The ultimate politician. Correction, as of last year, a retired politician, and that meant it was the first time in seventy years a Merrick hadn't been in the U.S. Senate.

And since her half brother Sloan refused to even think about leaving the family ranch and his lovely new wife, Jade, Alisa was the last of the Merricks to go into politics. To carry on the legacy.

"Maybe it might be a good idea to park your sports car," Clay said. "For a more sensible vehicle."

Alisa gasped. She loved that car.

Her father raised his hand. "Look, Alisa, if you're serious about this campaign you have to look and act the part. That hot rod isn't going to help you win votes, except with adolescent boys."

She had to give up her adventurous side. "I guess you're right. Just please don't make me drive a mini van."

Her father smiled. "I'm not making you drive anything. It's your decision, sweetheart. You asked for my input and I'm trying to advise you."

"Okay, I'll start driving one of the cars from the ranch." And she'd better not see her brother driving her beloved convertible, either.

Clay nodded his approval as he checked his list again. "Okay, you also need to reschedule the meeting you missed this morning. It's going to be the downtown shop owners who'll help get you elected."

Suddenly Matt Rafferty came to mind. No man had a right to look that sexy. Had he ever thought about her? Just because they'd had a hot and heavy weekend together didn't mean it had been memorable for him.

She shook away her wayward thoughts to get back on track.

"I thought I might go by each shop owner and talk to them individually," she told her father. "That way I could see what their biggest concerns are. What they expect from me as a council member."

"That's good, too," he agreed. "Since you're running against Gladys Peters. She has a lot of support and it doesn't seem to matter that she's stuck in the last century. It's good for you that her ideas for the town are to keep things the same. Your platform for restoring the south end of Main Street is an excellent idea. Bringing more revenue to Kerry Springs is needed badly."

She kept thinking about Matt. He had a great location for his business. Was he planning to update the outside of the property, too? "The Raffertys taking over Rory's Bar is a good thing."

He nodded. "They have an excellent location at the corner. It will be nice to have a more upscale restaurant in town, too."

"Upscale?"

Her dad smiled. "From what I hear from Sean, Matt's going to offer a better dinner menu and an updated dining area. It's just what this town needs."

Kerry Springs needed a lot of things. "I'd like to renovate and reopen the Boys and Girls Club."

Her father frowned. "That's an ambitious call especially with limited funds in the town's budget."

"I know, but there are so many kids who need this place to go after school and in the summer."

Then he smiled. "I could help you with a fundraiser and get the donations started, look into some federal grant money."

"Dad."

Clay Merrick wasn't listening. "I have friends in Austin."

She adored this man who'd always been there for her. "Dad, I appreciate all your help, but I need to do this on my own."

He nodded in agreement. "Is it okay to tell you that I'm so proud of you, and the work you've done as project manager on the Vista Verde project? You've come into your own, sweetie. Yet, you'll always be my little girl, so it's natural to want to help you."

Alisa stood, went to him and placed a kiss on his cheek. "And I love you for it. Your help has been so valuable to me, but if people are going to take me seriously, I need to do this on my own. I plan to get a bare-bones estimate for the repairs of the Boys and Girls Club before I even go to the council."

Her dad smiled. "Looks like you have a handle on this."

Alisa thought she had until she ran into Matt Rafferty. She looked at her dad. "Well, I am Clay Merrick's daughter. I learned from the best."

Later that day, Matt cursed as the pain in his shoulder kept him from finishing the trim. He didn't want to get behind schedule for the opening.

And if he kept letting Alisa Merrick disrupt his thoughts, he'd be losing more of both, time and money. Hell, what was wrong with him? She'd been back in town for months and it hadn't bothered him. They'd pretty much managed to stay out of each other's way.

Not that he should have gotten involved with her in the first place. Damn, a Merrick. What had he been thinking? He should have left her alone that night. That was the problem. He hadn't been thinking about anything except how Alisa felt in his arms, or how she tasted.

Their chance meeting at the Roadhouse Bar three years ago had been a fluke. He'd been home on leave from the army with time on his hands and feeling restless he'd gone out there for a few drinks. Alisa and a couple of her girlfriends from Austin had been out slumming when he saw them walk through the door of the rowdy country-western bar just outside of Kerry Springs. The element in the place was rough; mainly cowboys who wanted to let off a little steam and find someone to share the night. If lucky, a bed.

If he'd been smart, he would have minded his own business and finished his pool game. But when Billy and Cordell Jenkins started hitting on the ladies, he couldn't turn away. No way could he just sit by and let it happen. He wasn't that much of a jerk.

He'd managed to handle the situation without any bloodshed. It cost him a round of drinks for the two cowboys, but he got the women out of there. Alisa's friends went back to their hotel, but she ended up with him. She'd made no bones about how much she wanted him.

They'd ended up at her place, the old homestead at the Merrick Ranch. He'd spent the next two days in her bed. That had been the first rule he'd broken, never spend the entire night. Second, never talk about a future.

With Alisa, he'd lost count of all the broken rules. When he finally realized how hard he was falling for her, he'd made a quick exit. He couldn't let it go any further. He didn't do permanent. Not with a woman anyway.

Not since his mother walked out on him and his brother when they'd been kids. Not learning his lesson, he'd let it happened again in high school with steady girlfriend, Jody Haynes. Then she had cut him loose right before she'd left for college, leaving him behind when he'd lost his athletic scholarship because of an injury and a low GPA. That had been when Jody informed him she was going to find a man with a better future to give her the lifestyle she aspired to.

So for years, Matt played the dating games, but he let the women know the rules. Then Alisa Merrick had walked into his life, and every bit of common sense nearly flew out the window. So before Matt let it happen a third time, he managed to leave Alisa's bed. Okay, he was a coward and left before dawn and didn't even say goodbye.

He knew he couldn't face her hurt, but it had been the only way he could survive the coming year. Going overseas, he couldn't risk thinking about her, wondering if she'd be there when he got back. No, he wouldn't be vulnerable again. So he stood by his hard fast rule, and had been the first to leave.

Luckily he'd managed to return home from his tour of duty, but not without his problems. He'd seen things, gone through things that had changed him. No matter if they were invisible, he still had scars. Alisa had already caught a glimpse of his moment of despair. Even if he wanted a relationship with her, was he ready for one? Better yet, would she give him a second chance?

"Hey, are you slacking off again?"

Matt jumped and swung around to see his older brother, Evan. "I'm entitled to a break now and then."

Evan smiled. "You need some help?"

"The problems I got you can't help me with."

"Try me," Evan said.

Matt could only stare at his big brother. Evan had always been there for him. Those years after Patty Rafferty decided she didn't need two boys and a husband to tie her down and left, Evan had taken care of him.

"Don't you have a pretty wife and a couple of kids to get home to?"

He grinned at the mention of Jenny, Gracie and little Mick. "I can spare a few minutes for my brother."

Evan had married at a young age. He'd managed to survive a loveless union that had produced his daughter, Gracie. After Megan died, he buried himself in work trying to raise his child, then had Jenny come into his life and shown him real love.

"Come on," Evan went on, "you can take some time off. Let your body heal."

Work was all Matt had. "I need to get this done."

"Why? You can cover the mortgage even if you open after the original date." Evan frowned. "Is there something else bothering you?"

Matt shook his head.

"You sure? This has woman-trouble all over it."

Matt forced a laugh. "Just when would I have time for a woman? I've been working here day and night."

"I know my brother. You manage to find female companionship in the least likely places." He looked thoughtful. "But it does seem to me you've been without anyone in a while, unless you count this morning when a pretty woman was pacing the hospital waiting room."

Alisa was worried about him? "The only reason Alisa Merrick was worried about me was that it could cause her some bad press."

Evan folded his arms over his chest. "I sense it's more than that." He didn't stop. "You know, she'd be the prefect woman for you."

Matt tried not to react. "Oh, wise brother, please tell me why you'd think that."

"Best of all, she's not like your usual type. I doubt she'd take any of your guff. Kind of like Jenny."

He thought of Alisa and felt a twinge of longing. He quickly pushed it aside. "You forgot the most important thing, bro. Unlike you, I don't want to settle down."

CHAPTER THREE

THE next day, Alisa was kept busy making her way up
and down Main Street, trying to get votes and find out
what the store owners wanted. She got a variety of answers, but mostly they wanted more business downtown. The empty storefronts at the end of the street
worried them, too.

The wind whipped her hair and she brushed it back
as she made her way into Shaffer's Ice Cream Parlor to
pick up the key to the Boys and Girls Club.

Jaclyn Shaffer was behind the counter busy with customers. Her best friend since high school, Jacyln had
taken over running the shop after her parents retired
and moved to Florida. The tall, athletic blonde had been
the one who had talked Alicia into running for council
when she returned to Kerry Springs.

Her friend waved to her. "Give me a few minutes."

Alisa nodded. "Take your time."

Since Jaclyn had added a lunch menu, her business
had increased, especially the takeout orders from other
shop owners along Main. Plus with Rory's closed temporarily, she was even busier. Was Matt planning to be
open for lunch? She couldn't help but wonder how he
was doing today. Was his shoulder better?

She shook away the thought. Matt Rafferty could

take care of himself. He had his family to help him. The last thing she needed to do was go anywhere near him again.

Someone came into the shop and the strong wind blew the door open farther. Once it closed again, the middle-aged woman smoothed her hair. "It's getting nasty out there," she said. "There's a bad storm heading our way. We're under a tornado watch."

Alisa nodded, a little concerned. "That's springtime in Texas."

The woman added, "Well, as soon as I pick up my order, I'm headed home and into my basement."

Alisa glanced outside and saw dark, ominous clouds gathering. Maybe she should hurry things along, too, and get to the Boys and Girls Club. She went to the counter and got Jaclyn's attention. "Can I get the key to the club? I want to check out the building before this storm breaks."

Jaclyn glanced outside, reached under the counter and handed Alisa the key she'd gotten from the club's director. "Okay, I'll try to get down there, if I can get away."

Alisa hurried out of the shop and down two blocks passing the empty storefronts until she came to a brick building. A faded Boys and Girls Club was embossed on the double doors. She used the key and got inside just as the heavens opened up and the rain began to come down hard. Lightning flashed across the sky and the thunder rumbled loudly.

Alisa flinched, happy to be inside. She could wait out the storm here if need be.

Brushing off her short-sleeve blue sweater and navy skirt, she looked around. She hit the light switch to the reception area and could see there hadn't been any improvements made in years. The walls were dingy and the floors worn. She hit another switch as she walked down the hall past several rooms that seemed to be used now for storage. Then she made her way to the gymnasium. That was when she heard a noise. Someone was here. Who? The place had been closed indefinitely.

She peered through the window of the swinging doors. In the dim light there was someone dribbling a basketball at the other end of the court. She watched awhile before she recognized Matt.

Great. What was he doing here?

She watched as he did a series of dribbles with the ball, then took off and drove to the basket, dropping in a shot. Then another and another without pausing, or slowing down. It didn't seem his shoulder was bothering him now. She pushed through the door and walked along the edge of the room so as not to disturb him.

Matt continued the exercise over and over as if he were being chased. He kept up the pace, making jump shot after jump shot. Retrieving the ball, he went for another basket, picking up another ball and tossing it into the hoop.

Thunder roared outside, but there seemed to be a bigger storm brewing inside this man as if he were unable to stop. What was driving him so hard? Alisa was close enough to see the sweat dripping off him, but he still didn't stop. Then suddenly the silence was pierced with the sound of a siren.

A tornado sighting.

Matt froze, then swung around and saw her. "What the hell?" Dropping the ball, he hurried toward to her. "We need to take cover."

She froze. "Where?"

He grabbed her hand. "Come on." He pulled her along with him and into the hallway.

Matt didn't want to think about how long Alisa had been standing there, watching him. He hadn't exactly been aware of things going on around him. He was now, though, as the sound of the siren rang in his ears. Pulling Alisa along with him, he headed toward the section where the showers were, then suddenly the lights flashed and went out altogether. Ignoring Alisa's gasp, he pulled her into a dark room.

Another loud crash of thunder. "Don't worry, I know my way around here blindfolded."

He felt her hand shaking as he took her into the tiled room and up against the wall. The smell of mildew assaulted his nose.

Her breathing was rapid. "Shouldn't we go to the basement?"

"Not sure if we can get there from here. I for one don't want to take any chances roaming around trying to find the door. We should be safe here," he told her. "We're next to plumbing and an inside wall."

"Do you think the tornado will hit the town?"

He still grasped her hand, and he wasn't about to let go. "Not sure, and I'm not going to go looking to see."

"Good. Because I don't want you to leave me," she said, her voice breathless.

Suddenly the winds died outside and he didn't like that. Something was going to happen. He felt it in his bones.

"Is it over?"

"I wish. As they say, it's just the calm before the real storm." He slid down the wall, making her sit, too, wondering if there were any other precautions he could take. This wasn't just about him. He fought to stay in the moment, not to let anything bad take him away, to keep him from protecting Alisa.

He worked to stay focused. "What the hell were you doing out in this weather?" he asked her.

"I could ask you the same thing. Besides, this place has been locked up for months."

"There are ways to get in if you know where to look. Evan and I practically lived here as a kids. What about you?"

"I came to see what improvements are needed to help this place."

Suddenly the wind began to howl again, along with hail pounding the narrow window, high up on the wall. It was starting again. "There's a long list, darlin'."

"Well, I'd like to hear it. Maybe later when I'm not so…distracted."

"I won't let anything happen to you."

A loud noise, similar to a train coming toward them, drowned out their voices. Then the sound of splintering wood, and he pulled Alisa down and covered her body with his. A series of memories flooded his head, recalling their night together. Her shapely body alive under his, those seductive sounds coming from her sweet mouth.

Her arms tightened around his back, pressing him even closer. "Oh, Matt," she whispered in his ear. "I'm scared."

"It's going to be okay, Alisa." He felt her tremble. Good Lord, help me. He closed his eyes for what seemed like an eternity as the storm played with the roof of the building, making enough noise to seem like it was being torn away. Finally the storm seemed to dissipate and move on, leaving silence, then the heavy rain started in its wake.

Alisa felt him tense, the drumming of his heart, and the sweat that beaded along his body. She drew back, and cupped his face in her hands.

Even though the light was dim, she could see the blank look in his eyes. "Stay with me, Matt," she called to him. "Come on. It's almost over."

He blinked and looked down at her. Damn. He'd done it again. He worked to adjust to the darkness and he found Alisa staring back at him. His chest tightened with a need he hadn't felt in a long time.

"It seems we're safe," she said a little breathlessly.

"No, we're definitely still in danger." Unable to re-sist, he leaned down and took her mouth in a deep, I'm-happy-to-be-alive kiss. Alisa wasn't stopping him, either. He cupped the back of her head, then angled her mouth to deepen the kiss. He pressed his tongue against her lips, causing her to open for him. Then she made a soft whimpering sound, he was lost in her. God help him, he was only human.

He finally broke off the kiss. She looked as dazed as he felt. He couldn't find any words, so he did what any red-blooded male would do when there was a beautiful woman in his arms. He leaned back down and kissed her again.

It wasn't until he heard someone calling her name that he tore his mouth away. His breathing was rough when he said, "I'd say they got here just in time."

Alisa managed to get to her feet as Matt called out to their rescuers. He took her hand and started back to-ward the hall. They saw a beam from a flashlight, then Jaclyn hurried to her. "Alisa!"

"I'm here."

Her friend hugged her just as Sheriff Bradshaw arrived.

Jaclyn stood back. "Oh, my, God. Are you all right?"

She had to look away. "I'm fine. Just frightened. Matt took me into the shower area." She glanced over her shoulder at the makeshift bunker. "So it really was a tornado?"

The sheriff nodded. "You were lucky. Just touched down once, there's roof damage here and next door." Bradshaw studied Alisa and Matt. "You sure you're both okay?"

Matt nodded. "That was a little close for comfort though."

"I agree." The sheriff turned back to Alisa. "I'm sure your daddy would appreciate a call from you."

Alisa had known the sheriff most of her life. The middle-aged man was well liked in town. "As soon as I get my cell phone."

Bradshaw nodded. "Unless you need me, I've got to check the rest of downtown for damage."

She waved him off. "We're fine."

She stole a glance at Matt. His smoldering gaze bore into hers, then he nodded. "I'd better get back to see if there's a roof on my building." He turned and walked out.

Alisa looked back at Jaclyn who was smiling. "What?"

"Only you would manage to get trapped in a tornado with none other than Matt Rafferty."

"It wasn't as if I went looking for him. He was here playing basketball when I came inside." Her heart rate still hadn't slowed to normal. "What was I supposed to do?"

"It seems that you can't help it. You two are like a

couple of magnets. That's twice in less than forty-eight hours that you two have tangled."

Jaclyn had been the only person Alisa confided in about what had happened between her and Matt three years ago.

"It looks like fate wants you together."

"Well, I'm going to ignore it. I have no time for Matt Rafferty."

Her friend groaned. "For that hunk of pure male, I'd make time."

"No, Jaclyn. I don't want to be grouped in with his long list of women. Besides, he didn't want me the first time. Why would I think that would change now?"

She started walking toward the hall, and found her purse, recalling the time when Matt first came home from the army. She'd been working in Austin. He'd called her, but the second she'd seen his number, she let it go to voice mail. She erased the message without listening to it. She was still too vulnerable, too hurt. He never called back.

Her friend caught up with her. "All I know is how he was looking at you just now."

It had been a long time since Alisa stopped wishing it could have been different between them.

She wasn't ready to take that chance with Matt, even if his kisses made her breathless. "Again, I don't have time for a man. All my extra time is set aside to concentrate on my job at AC Construction and my campaign, which you're supposed to be helping me with."

"And I am. I just thought…"

"That's past history, Jaclyn. Matt Rafferty has no place in my future." Now if she could only believe her own words.

* * *

Matt had cut through the alley and made it back to his place in minutes. He busied himself with checking for any leaks in the roof and windows. He couldn't afford to replace anything more right now. By the looks of things, the place didn't have any damage from the storm. He'd lucked out this time.

He sat down at the bar. Not so lucky was finding Alisa at the club. It had been the one place he could go and burn off some tension and frustration. The woman had caused him both.

The kiss. Hell, it was practically an assault on her mouth. His body got all stirred up just thinking about how she felt in his arms, how sweet she tasted. Some things a man never forgets. That had been one of the memories that he'd taken with him overseas. No one tasted as sweet and as tempting as Alisa Merrick. Trouble was she was the one woman who had gotten too close to burning him. He couldn't give her a second chance at it. He'd never let another woman play his heart.

A sudden noise in the back room caught his attention. He listened closely. It was the sound of the rain, but something nagged at him. He got off the bar stool and started toward the kitchen. He opened the swinging door and found the huge stainless steel refrigerator door ajar, blocking whoever was searching inside. The only thing he saw was a pair of feet in beat-up sneakers. The door hid the rest of the miniature thief.

Silently Matt moved across the empty kitchen, reached around and grabbed the kid by the back of his shirt.

"Hey, let me go," the young boy yelled as he kicked and swung his arms to get free.

Matt was strong enough to hold tight. "Why should I when I catch you stealing from me?"

"You got nothing to steal, so let me go."

Unable to confine the kid's swinging arms, he picked him up and set him down on the countertop. "Settle down, I only want to talk to you."

The kid looked to be about nine years old. "You'll call the sheriff and I'll end up in juvie hall."

Matt had gotten the same threat as a kid. "No, I promise I won't call any authority."

Finally the kid with the dirty blond hair and face looked up at him with big brown eyes. "Why should I believe you?"

"Because I don't lie to kids. What's your name?"

"Who wants to know?"

"Matt Rafferty."

"C.J." He glanced around. "Where's Rory?"

"In Florida. He sold the place—to me."

"Oh." The kid looked him over. "You know Sean?"

Matt nodded. "He's my dad. How do you know him?"

"Sometimes he and Rory let me help clean up the kitchen."

Matt hadn't heard his dad talk about any kid. "You hungry?"

"Maybe, but you ain't got nothin' here."

Matt opened a cupboard and pulled out a loaf of bread, then reached into the cupboard for peanut butter and grape jelly. "How about a sandwich?"

"I guess," the boy said, but his eyes just about bugged out of his head when he spotted the food.

Matt took out four slices of bread and began to spread the peanut butter. After the sandwich was made he started to hand it to the boy. "Wash your hands."

C.J. didn't argue, just went to the large sink. Finished,

he wiped his hands on his filthy jeans. Matt gave him the prize and watched as the boy devoured it in two bites.

Matt found a can of soda on the shelf in the refrigerator. He popped the top and handed it to the boy. "Where are your parents, C.J.?"

The kid took a long drink, then said, "Around. Why are you asking so many questions?"

Matt pulled out a stool and sat down. "Well, since you ended up at my place, and you're a minor, I want to make sure you have a place to stay."

The kid studied him. "The Wagon Wheel Trailer Park."

Not sure if he believed the boy, but the trailer park was well-known for its temporary residents. "Is your dad working the ranches?"

C.J. started on the second sandwich. "Yeah. That's right, he's working the roundup."

Matt started to speak but heard his name called out, then the kitchen door swung open and Alisa Merrick walked in. She didn't look happy. "Okay, Rafferty, we need to talk."

C.J. stood and grabbed the rest of his sandwich and soda. "I'm out of here." Before Matt could stop him, the kid ran out the back door.

He hurried after him. "Wait, C.J.," he called into the empty alley. "Damn." He came back inside to see Alisa.

"Sorry," she said. "I didn't know there was anyone here."

"Well, he's gone now." Strange, but he hoped that the boy would be back.

"Who is he?"

Matt shook his head. "Not sure." He was afraid he might be a runaway.

He looked at Alisa. She had changed into a white Western blouse and a pair of faded jeans. She might have covered those shapely legs, but he'd never forget them.

"What brings you by?" He tossed her a grin. "Can't get enough of me, huh?"

Alisa wanted to wipe that grin off his face, knowing he was trying to make her disappear. Well, she wasn't going anywhere until she had her say.

"I've had more than enough of you, Matt Rafferty. In fact more than I need. And that kiss earlier…that wasn't a good idea. Don't think that changes anything between us."

He strolled over to her. She had to fight to stand her ground. "And now, here I thought it was an enjoyable experience," he said.

"Well, you thought wrong. That weekend we spent together was a long time ago. It wouldn't be wise for either one of us to start anything now."

"Was that what you were trying to tell me earlier when you were crawling all over me?"

She held her temper, just barely. "There was a tornado. If anything, you were taking advantage."

He shrugged. "If you say so."

Oh, this man infuriated her, but she couldn't let him see that. "So we agree to stay out of each other's way?"

"It seems to be safer for me if I stay out of your path. No telling what's going to happen next with you around."

She forced a smile. "All the more reason to avoid each other."

"Okay," he agreed. "I'll make sure I cross the street if I see you. We wouldn't want people to know that you ever associated with the likes of me."

"That's not what I meant. It's just that I have a campaign to run. Being on the town council is important to me."

He studied her with those deep blue eyes. "Yep, that's right, we're your stepping stone to Washington D.C."

CHAPTER FOUR

NEARLY a week later, Alisa's alarm went off and she dragged herself out of bed. This morning she had to dig deep for some enthusiasm to start off her day. She walked out of the master bedroom though the two bedroom town home toward the open kitchen area.

The place had been her dad's during his years in the Senate. Mostly it was for staff and visitors. Since Alisa returned home, she'd moved in here to be closer to her job on the Vista Verde project. Since Clay's retirement, he didn't need his office space, either, so he gladly let her. As much as she loved living in the homestead house at the ranch, she also liked being close to her friends and work. They'd been doing preliminary work on phase II of Vista Verde. As project manager, she had worked long hours.

AC Construction's first section of affordable homes had sold immediately, and there was already a waiting list for the next twenty-four. Rancher Alex Casali had the money and vision to fund the affordable housing project. This coming week they were scheduled to pour the foundations, unless there was bad weather or any other setback.

No! No setbacks. She wouldn't allow it. She'd gotten all the bids from the subcontractors and it was pretty much the same crew as before. She knew they were dependable and did a great job.

So she didn't need any distractions like Matt Rafferty. Her thoughts turned to how he held her during the storm. The kisses that had kept her awake more than she wanted to admit. Why? Why couldn't she just let it go? He was not a good bet except for heartbreak. Again.

She needed to stay focused. No time to think about a man. With only five weeks left until the elections, she'd already clocked a ton of miles going door to door for votes. She'd already asked Alex for a bid on the repairs for the Boys and Girls Club. Then she could announce how they could raise money to get the improvements made. It would be her first order of business, if she won a seat on the council. So Matt Rafferty wasn't welcome in her thoughts, or in her future. Those dreams had long since died.

She carried her coffee through the French doors that led to the second-story balcony. The town house was just off Main Street and overlooked the city park. She loved the quiet, simple view. All the trees were coming to life and the grass was recovering from the long cold winter. It was early morning, but there were people out. She smiled, seeing a few runners making their way around the park.

After a few minutes of calming solitude, she started to return inside when she spotted another figure through the trees. A kid? What was a kid doing in the park by himself when it wasn't even seven in the morning? She watched as he walked toward the trash can and began going through it. He pulled out several aluminum soda cans and put them in his backpack. He continued through the next few trash bins. Finally the boy got close enough for her to recognize his jacket and blond head. Was he the child who was in Matt's kitchen?

Where were his parents? She went back inside, showered and got dressed, but before heading to work she took a detour through the park. By the time she got there the boy was gone. What should she do now?

After a dreamless night's sleep, Matt had been up at five. No flashbacks. No nightmares. Smiling, he fed the livestock and did his chores, then headed into town. He had a full day planned as he was trying to hire a bartender, a cook and three waitresses.

This was all so new to him. He knew how to handle ranch hands, but how did you hire a good waitress? His dad suggested he rehire Shirley and Kim, two long-time waitresses who'd worked for Rory. And if he needed help with any other future employees to call him.

Matt agreed to the idea. With his arms filled with bags, he managed to unlock the back door and walk into the kitchen. He brought food hoping his young friend, C.J., would stop by. He put milk, cold cuts and yogurt in the refrigerator. He placed cans of soup in the cupboard with a fresh loaf of bread and some sweet rolls, then left the door unlocked as an invitation.

Matt heard a sound and turned around to see the door open and Alisa walk in. His heart sped up a little. Damn, if she didn't look good first thing in the morning. A fitted soft blue blouse tucked into a pair of pleated trousers. Her nearly black hair was pulled back into a ponytail, exposing her pretty face. Those big, midnight-blue eyes. Those full lips that made his own mouth water.

"Before you get angry, I'm only here to ask you a

question about the little boy who was here the other day."

"Morning to you, too, Alisa."

"Sorry. Morning, Matt."

"So what questions do you have about C.J.?"

"That's his name?"

Matt shrugged. "That's all I could get out of him. Why?"

"I was out on my condo balcony this morning and saw him—I'm almost positive it was him." Her gaze locked on his. "He was going through the trash cans in the park."

"Damn, I was afraid of that."

"So you haven't seen him again?"

"Not since that one day. I stocked the refrigerator with food, hoping he'd come by again."

"You think he's homeless?"

"He told me he and his dad live at the Wagon Wheel Trailer Park."

She nodded. "Then that's where I'll start. Thanks."

She turned to leave, but he stopped her. "Hey, you're going over there?"

"Yes. A child can't just wander the streets."

This had been the last thing he expected. "I'll go with you."

She shook her head. "You don't need to."

The hell he didn't. "Being a former resident, I might be able to help." And he didn't want her going alone into that environment, he added silently. Not waiting for an argument, he escorted her out the door. She walked ahead to an SUV.

He was surprised. "Where's the sports car?"

"It's not always practical. This is better for work."

"So is it safe to ride with you?"

"You're just full of it, Rafferty."

He grinned. "And you're so easy to rile." He climbed into the passenger's side and fastened his seat belt. "Okay, let's go find a kid."

Ten minutes later, they pulled into a parking spot at the office of the trailer park at the edge of town. It was worse than Matt remembered. It had been years since he'd lived here with his dad and Evan. It had been the only place Sean Rafferty could afford while raising two small boys on his own after his wife took off with all their money and their only car.

If possible, the place was even more run-down. The rental trailers looked in worse shape then they had twenty-five years ago. The landscaping was nothing but dirt and weeds. And that wasn't the only kind of weed you could find here. He knew about a few drug busts that had taken place on the premises.

He opened the door. "Let's get this over with."

Alisa climbed out, too. Although it was uncomfortable being with Matt she was glad he was with her. They went inside the office and immediately the smell of cigarettes and alcohol hit her. She had to breathe slowly to keep from getting sick.

An old man came out of the back room with a week's growth of whiskers, dressed in a dirty T-shirt and jeans. He looked them over. "We don't rent on a daily basis. Go to the motel out on the highway."

She heard Matt curse under his breath. "We don't want to rent, just have a few questions."

The guy's eyes narrowed. "You the law?"

She could see Matt wasn't exactly calm. "No, we're concerned about a child." He pulled out some bills from his front pocket and laid them on the counter. "A blond-headed kid about nine. Calls himself C.J."

The guy eyed the twenties, then swept them up. "Yeah, C.J. used to live here, but his dad packed up and moved on a few weeks ago."

"What about the mother? Did she move somewhere else in town?"

"No old lady. As long as they pay the rent on time, it's not my business where they go."

Feeling Matt tense, Alisa jumped in and asked. "Do you know the boy's full name?"

He shrugged. "Dad's name was Charlie Jackson. The kid, not sure. I just figured the initials stood for Charlie junior."

Matt nodded. "Thanks."

Alisa felt Matt's hand on her lower back as they headed out the door. They made it back to the car and got in. She turned to him. "You think that C.J. and his dad are living in their car, or on the street?"

"I don't know. Only the kid can answer that."

"We have to find him."

Matt checked his watch. "Not if he doesn't want to be found. So I'm going back to work."

"Don't you even care—"

His glare stopped her words. "Hell, yes I care. I know what it's like to live hand-to-mouth. But I also know a thing about pride, too. From what I learned from the kid, he used to help out at the bar when Rory owned it. He doesn't want charity. My hope is he'll come back."

He saw her eyes well up. "So he goes hungry."

"I stocked up with some food. Now I need to get back in case he shows."

She nodded. "Okay. But I'm going to keep looking for him."

"He's a smart kid, Alisa." He reached across the car and brushed her cheek. "We'll find him," he assured her. "I'm going to do everything possible to see that he's safe."

Over the next twenty-four hours, Matt put out some bait hoping C.J. would show up at the restaurant. He'd left the back door unlocked while he worked out front, but so far nothing.

Not discouraged, Matt went back to interviewing applicants.

"Kevin Ross," he said as a young man walked through the front door at the bar.

"That's me."

The applicant was a thirty-something man in dark trousers and a collared shirt. He wore his short brown hair in a military cut.

"How long have you been out of the service?" Matt asked.

"I was discharged in January."

Matt glanced over Ross's résumé, showing he'd spent ten years in the army, stationed in Germany with the second Stryker division. Did two deployments to Afghanistan.

"I've been out eighteen months," Matt told him, wondering if Kevin suffered any repercussions.

Ross nodded. "Thought I'd get out and marry my girl, but by the time I got home, she'd already replaced me."

"Yeah, man, that's rough."

Kevin shook his head. "The way I see it, I dodged a bullet. So now, I'm going to college during the day, and hoping I can find a job working evenings. To be honest, I'm not exactly experienced, but I took a bartending course and I'm a quick study."

Matt decided right off that this guy wouldn't let him down. "I figure you served our country, you're capable of serving a few drinks. My dad is the best there is, but he wants to retire. He'll be helping out for a while in the first few weeks, he can teach you more about being behind the bar than anyone I know."

"There's one other thing. I've been going to counseling…ever since I've gotten back." He hesitated. "I've had a lot to adjust to."

Matt knew exactly what he was talking about. "Do you think it will affect your work?"

He shook his head. "Mainly my sleep. Nightmares. I felt you needed to know."

"I appreciate you telling me. Any problem starting next week?"

"I'm hired?"

Matt nodded and handed him his business card. "Come in next week to train and we'll work around your classes."

They shook hands. "I won't let you down," Kevin said.

"I don't expect you will."

Matt watched Kevin through the window as he met up with a friend. Looked like a brother. He smacked him on the back and they walked off together.

"Glad I could make someone's day." He thought back to Kevin talking about his counseling. Nightmares. Matt remembered a time when he first came home, he had trouble deciphering what was real and what was fiction. He spent weeks in group therapy. It helped. It even helped more coming back home. Then the past few weeks, seemed that the nightmares had increased. Stress.

Suddenly Alisa came to mind. She'd seen more of his condition. He didn't like feeling exposed to her. He wasn't the same man who'd walked away from her three years ago. He might never be. So what? It wasn't like he wanted to start up a relationship with her.

Something stirred deep in his gut, and he quickly brushed off the feelings. Okay, he hadn't seen her in two days, and he'd kind of missed her hanging around. Not good. He didn't need Alisa Merrick messing up his head. He needed to concentrate on opening this restaurant.

He walked into the kitchen and found the boy sitting at the counter. "So you decided to come back."

That afternoon, Alisa walked into the Blind Stitch Quilt Shop and found Jenny Rafferty behind the counter. With a wave, Alisa walked through the busy shop, and into the connecting storefront that was the classroom. In the front, by the windows was the large round table around which sat her mother, along with her friends, Millie, Beth and Liz. She was surprised to see her sister-in-law, Jade. A nurse on staff at the medical center, she hadn't been much of a quilter. Maybe Mother had finally talked her into it.

Her mother spotted her. "Alisa. What a surprise."

"I always know where to find you."

The older woman stood and hugged her. "I'm only here a few days a week. Your father and I were going to stop by the construction site and see you later."

Was her father up to something? "Is there a problem?"

"No, I believe this has to do with organizing a fund-raiser."

Alisa wasn't excited about using her father to get on

the council. "Mom, I told Dad I wanted to do this my-self."

Louisa shook her head. "No, this has to do with the Boys and Girls Club."

Beth jumped in. "I think it's wonderful that you want to fix up the place. It's a disgrace that's it's gotten so run-down. Our kids deserve better." The older woman frowned. "In fact it was Gladys who helped close the club last year, saying there wasn't any money in the budget."

"Really?" Alisa said. "That's interesting."

Millie stood up from the table. "You know what else is interesting? We seemed to have the money to fix the drainage system on the town golf course. Excuse me, I've got to go and relieve Jenny from the cash register so she can feed Mick."

Alisa was happy she was getting support for her proj-ect. "So you all think it's worth reopening?"

They all said a united "Yes."

"And we're going to help," Liz said. "We're going to donate two quilts for a raffle."

"There's more." Beth's eyes lit up. "Sean said Evan was going to donate some of the profits from the grand opening of Rafferty's Place."

"That's so generous."

"It was actually Matt's idea," Beth added.

"Isn't it wonderful," her mother said. "Old Gladys is going to have a cow."

"Mother, I haven't won the election, yet," Alisa ar-gued. "You might have to continue to deal with her."

Beth patted her hand. "Oh, sweetheart, I have a feel-ing once people hear about your intention they'll be lin-ing up to vote for you."

A smiling Jenny started across the room. She wasn't

alone, Matt was next to her, walking his nephew, Mick. Finally he hauled the hefty toddler up into his arms and continued the journey. The boy's arms went around his uncle's neck and hugged him close.

Alisa's heart shot off as they approached. He looked so natural with the child.

"Good to see you, Alisa, especially on foot," he said. "I feel much safer."

"Funny, Rafferty." It had been a few days and she found she'd missed seeing him. Darn it. "Be careful, my car is parked at the curb."

"Thanks for the warning."

She had to stop looking at this man. "Hello, Mick."

The boy gave her a toothy grin and reached for her. She caught the toddler in her arms. "Oh, my, you're such a big boy."

The child was now fascinated with her necklace and Matt was watching her intently. She was feeling uncomfortable with the attention.

"Beth just told me about your generous donation for the Boys and Girls Club," she said. "Thank you."

Those deep blue eyes locked on hers. "I'm fond of the place. It holds special memories for me."

Alisa felt a warm tingle down her spine. "I know you spent a lot of time there as a kid. Maybe you'll think about volunteering once the place is up and running again."

He only smiled. "Maybe. Right now, I need to get back to work." He leaned forward to kiss his stepmother, Beth, and placed a noisy kiss on his nephew's cheek. He was very close to Alisa. "I need to talk to you," he said softly. "It's about C.J."

"You found him? Where?"

"Come by the restaurant." He stepped back, and

waved to everyone. After a quick word with his sister-in-law, Jenny, he left the shop.

Alisa wanted to follow him, but if she did there would be questions to answer. She couldn't get tangled up with Matt.

"How about some lunch?" her mother asked, bringing her back to the present.

"Sorry, Mom, I can't," Alisa told her. "I really need to get back to my work, too."

After answering a few questions about the Verde Vista project, Alisa handed little Mick back to his mother, said her goodbyes and then out the door. Once in her car, she drove around the block and parked on a side street then walked to Rafferty's Place from the alley.

Inside the kitchen, she spotted the twosome at the counter. C.J. spotted her first. "Are you gonna send me to jail?"

His dirty face and clothes made her want to cry. "No, I'd like to help you."

"I don't want any help. I'm fine on my own." He turned those big brown eyes toward Matt. "Aren't I, Matt?"

"Sure, son." He put his hand on the boy's shoulder. "But remember, you promised you'd listen to what we have to say."

C.J. glared back at Alisa. "What is she, your old lady?"

Matt grinned. "You better get your eyes checked, kid," he said. "Alisa definitely isn't old." She felt his gaze move over her. "But I'd say she's definitely a lady, and a beautiful one."

CHAPTER FIVE

Alisa ignored Matt's flirting and pulled him toward the far side of the kitchen. "Okay, now that C.J.'s here, what are we going to do?"

"I hadn't thought that far ahead," he told her.

"One thing for sure, you can't give the boy back to a man who deserted him. What kind of parent abandons his own child?"

Seeing Matt stiffen, she suddenly realized the implication of her words. "Matt, I'm sorry. I didn't mean…"

"Forget it." He brushed it aside. "My childhood is old news." His gaze never left her. "I would never send the kid back to his old man. Maybe there's a relative who can take him?"

"And in the meantime?"

"Get him cleaned up and feed him." Matt folded his arms across his chest. "You don't have to worry, Alisa, I'll handle it."

"Wait a minute. You're talking about breaking the law."

"I'm just buying a little time."

"Matt, C.J. is a minor and he's all alone. The authorities have to be contacted."

"I know all about how the authorities will handle

this. A foster home, or a group home with other badass kids. C.J. will never get out of the system."

How bad had Matt's childhood been? "That's not for us to decide. We need to let the sheriff know what's going on."

Matt combed his fingers through his hair. "That gets rid of the problem, doesn't it? I thought you wanted to make things better for kids. Or was that all talk?"

That hurt, but Alisa refused to let him see that. "Okay, what do you want me to do?"

At first he didn't say anything, then blurted out, "I was thinking he could go home with me—at least for tonight. C.J. trusts me."

"Social Services will still need to be notified."

"Not right now." He lowered his voice. "Look, they probably don't have room in a foster home, anyway."

He was probably right, but still… "How can you finish the work here and open this place in less than two weeks while you're watching the boy?"

"I'll manage."

Matt glanced across the room to the boy. The truth was he wasn't sure he could do this. There were days he didn't feel he could handle himself. "Maybe I can do it temporarily. I have my own place at the ranch."

"Wouldn't it cramp your style?"

He couldn't hide his frustration. "What is it with you and my love life?"

A blush spread over her cheeks. "You can't deny there have been a lot of women in your life."

She drove him crazy. "I'm sorry I hurt you, Alisa. Back then I wasn't thinking about anything but getting through the day…and the nights."

She raised a hand. "You're right. I have no business rehashing the past. I won't bring it up again."

Looking at her now, Matt wasn't sure he could stop himself. "Agreed."

"You still can't do this on your own."

He shrugged. "I thought I'd get help…from you."

"Me?" She shook her head.

"Come on, Alisa. I can't turn my back on the boy." He swung around to head back to C.J. but the kitchen was empty. "Damn."

Alisa followed Matt out the door and into the alley. There was no sign of the boy. "Well, it looks like there isn't a problem on what to do now." He turned to her. "Now you can go home happy, Ms. Town Council Candidate. Your record is still spotless."

His words hurt her. "I'm not going anywhere. There's a boy out there who's too young to be by himself." She sighed. "There's some daylight left, so let's go find him."

Matt didn't move. "Why? So you can turn him over to the sheriff?"

She knew the important thing was to find the boy. "If we find him then I promise I won't say anything to the sheriff at least until we get the chance to locate a relative."

He smiled, and her pulse kicked into overdrive. He came toward her. "Really?"

He was watching her so intently she had to glance away. "C.J. needs people on his side." She wrinkled her nose. "Besides, I don't like being called an old lady. I need to straighten him out about that."

Matt couldn't stop the grin, but he was smart enough not to make any further comment. He grabbed Alisa's hand and they began to search the blocks in the area. As best as he could see, the empty storefronts didn't have a kid camped inside. They checked the park again, then as the sun was fading, they took one more sweep through the alleys. That was when they spotted the kid behind the Boys and Girls Club.

Matt pulled Alisa out of sight, then he saw C.J. go through a high window, just open enough for a child to get through. "Not this time, kid," he murmured as he tugged Alisa along with him.

Matt and Alisa made their way to the side door of the building. He took out his pocketknife and went to work on the flimsy lock. Once the door popped open, he stepped inside and waited for his eyes to adjust to the dim light.

"Can you see?" he whispered to Alisa.

"Yes," she whispered. "Let's just find the boy."

Silently he led her through the area, stopping to look for any signs of C.J., then he heard sounds coming from a room at the end of hall.

Inside the door there were several boxes stacked up high, but a dim light on the other side helped lead them through the maze. At the end they found an open area with shelves filled with books and stacks of clothing. A small wooden crate held a small lamp and a clock. There was a makeshift bed made out of piles of blankets.

Matt's chest tightened when he saw C.J. was sitting in the middle, eating the food he'd taken from the kitchen.

This was worse than he thought. Where the hell was his dad? As if the boy sensed he wasn't alone, he turned around. There was a frightened look in his eyes and Matt knew exactly how he felt.

"So this is home sweet home."

* * *

Half an hour later, all three of them were back at the restaurant. C.J. was reluctant, but Matt had seated the sullen boy at the counter.

Alisa frowned. His thin body bothered her.

"You can't make me stay here," C.J. said.

"No, I could turn you over to the sheriff," he told him.

That was the first sign of fear Alisa saw in the boy's eyes. "I didn't do anything," the kid argued. "My daddy's comin' back. He promised. You'll see."

Matt sat down on the stool beside him. "Until he does you still can't live on your own. How do you feel about coming home with me for a while?"

There was a flicker of hope in the child's eyes, then he glanced at Alisa. "What about her? She gonna tell on me?"

"Not unless you keep calling me an old lady."

Those brown eyes challenged her. "Well, don't you belong to him?"

"I don't belong to anyone."

"Then why are you two always lookin' at each other? You know, kinda funny like?"

Alisa didn't like where this was going. "Why don't we worry about getting you cleaned up, and see where we go from here."

"Home with me," Matt insisted.

Alisa knew Matt wasn't going to like her idea. She couldn't keep this a secret. What if C.J. was sick? "May I speak with you?"

Matt stood. "Don't think about running again," he said to C.J.

Once across the room at the back door, she said, "Maybe he should be checked out by a doctor." At

Matt's glare, she added. "Okay, how about if Jade looks at him? She's a nurse."

"Should we get her involved?"

"Matt, we need to get more help for the child. If you think about it, you'll know I'm right."

He folded his arms. "What's your idea?"

"We need to call someone who has connections. We need to call my dad."

An hour later, with the sun setting, Matt sat in his truck as he drove C.J. to the Merrick Ranch. How had he let Alisa talk him into this? Not that he had a chance once she'd gotten out her phone and called the senator. Things were set into motion even before he knew what had happened. The so-called plan was for everyone to meet at Alisa's house at the ranch.

He glanced to the backseat to find C.J. eating the second hamburger he'd bought before taking the thirty-mile trip out of town. They came to the high, wrought-iron gate that protected the property. He pressed the button and, once he gave his name, was allowed access. Driving along the road toward the main house, he veered off toward the right and up over the rise about a half mile toward the original homestead that had been Alisa's great-grandparents' home. Her great-grandfather had built the house when they first settled in the area. He'd heard from his father that now the house belonged to Alisa. It had been recently renovated so she could live in it.

Everyone in town knew the stories of Merrick history. Over a hundred years ago, the Kerry family and the Merrick family teamed up and built their dynasty. They'd made their money in cattle and smart investments.

A Rafferty could never compete with the Merricks' wealth and notoriety. He'd been crazy to spend time with Alisa three years ago. Coming back to the scene of the crime might be the second.

He pulled up in front of the white clapboard house. It had recently been restored, with a new roof and painted outside. The small porch had been rebuilt. It looked a lot different from when they'd spent that weekend here.

"Alisa lives here? Hey, this is cool," C.J. said from the back.

"Yeah. This is her parents' ranch."

"She must be rich."

"I guess you could say that," he murmured.

Just then car headlights appeared on the road. Alisa. She parked next to him, and got out. Soon after, another truck appeared. "Looks like the troops have arrived." He climbed out and helped C.J.

Alisa took several bags from the back as her brother, Sloan, and his new wife, Jade, pulled up in a truck.

"Hey, C.J.," Alisa said, carrying several sacks toward the front door. She reached inside the front door and turned on the porch light as the couple got out of their vehicle.

"Hey, Matt," Sloan called, walking up to him. "How's it going?"

"Hi, Sloan. Jade." He shook their hands. "I guess your sister filled you in on everything?"

Sloan gave a sideways glance at Alisa. "As well as she explains things."

Alisa stepped up. "Sloan, Jade, this is C.J."

Everyone exchanged greetings and Alisa led them inside. When she flipped on the lights Matt's head was flooded with memories. Although the room had been remodeled, the fireplace reminded him of the night there had been a big, roaring fire that had kept them cozy warm while they made love throughout the night. Whoa. He quickly shook away the thoughts and removed his hat.

Jade carried a small medical bag to the kitchen table. "Hey, C.J. you want to listen to your heart?" the pretty brunette said as she pulled out her stethoscope. The kid seemed okay with letting her check him out. Matt glanced at Sloan and caught big brother checking him out, too. Great that was all he needed now.

Twenty minutes later, C.J. had been examined by Nurse Jade, and though on the slim side, deemed healthy. So Alisa gave him the new clothes she'd purchased in town and sent him off to start a bath. She knew he was nine years old and probably able to wash himself, but Matt went in with him and supervised the boy's hygiene habits. Hearing the laughter through the door made her smile.

This was the easy part. Seeing the look on Sloan's face, she knew she was about to get his third degree.

"You want to tell me what's going on?" Sloan asked.

"I've already explained."

"But you didn't tell me about Matt. What's going on between the two of you?"

She refused to take the bait. "Nothing, except we found C.J." She embellished the truth a little. "When I stopped by the Raffertys' new restaurant to discuss the fundraiser they offered to do for the Boys and Girls Club, I saw the boy there. When he ran off, we joined forces to look for him."

Her half brother was the best big brother ever. He'd

been eight years old when Louisa married Senator Clay Merrick. He ran the family ranch, the River's End.

"Do you think it's wise to get involved with a runaway? I mean with the campaign."

"C.J. isn't a runaway, he was left behind by his father. The boy was living in an abandoned building, for God's sake.

"You could have called the authorities?"

"Boy, aren't you all warm and fuzzy. I thought Jade had softened you up."

"So did I," his wife chimed in. "Come on, Sloan, you'd do the same thing. Did you see how thin the child is? He needs an extra seven to ten pounds. If Matt can't take him in, I'm thinking we should."

"Whoa." He raised a hand. "We can't do that now, not with your job and the bab—"

Alisa stared at them. "Oh, you're going to have a baby!"

"Shh," Jade warned. "We haven't told anyone yet." She turned to her husband. "We're going to tell Louisa and Dad this weekend. So keep it to yourself for now."

Alisa hugged her. "You'll be great parents." Then she hugged her brother. "Of course, I'll be around to make sure he or she gets spoiled, too."

"I can't wait," Sloan groaned. "Back to the problem at hand. There could be some legal issues here, sis."

"We couldn't take him to the sheriff, Sloan. What if they sent him to a group home? I at least wanted to wait to hear what Dad says first."

Reluctantly Sloan agreed, then the couple left. It was a few minutes later that Matt brought a jean-clad boy out. Alisa took him into her bedroom to watch television.

When she returned, Matt was watching her. "I take

it your brother wasn't happy with this arrangement. He doesn't like me hanging around his baby sister."

Before she could say anything, the next visitor arrived, her dad.

Clay went to his daughter and they exchanged a hug. "Sorry it took so long, I had to wait on a phone call."

She gave him a nervous smile and glanced at Matt. "I appreciate that you want to help."

"Problem is, you might not like the solution I have for you." He looked at Matt and held out his hand. "Matt, it's good to see you again." Then they shook hands, then looked down the hall as the child came out of her bedroom. "This must be C.J."

The child nodded.

"Hello, C.J., I'm Clay Merrick. Everyone calls me Senator."

"Are you going to take me to jail?"

Her father crouched down in front of the boy. "No, son, no one is going to take you to jail." He glanced up at Matt. "I hear you want to stay with this guy."

The child's head bobbed up and down. "He said I could."

"Well, I can vouch that Matt Rafferty is a good guy. A war hero, too."

"C.J., why don't you go into the kitchen, Jade brought over some cookies." Once the boy walked off, she turned back to her Dad. "What did you find out? Can C.J. stay with Matt until they locate a relative?"

Senator nodded. "Yes, the boy can stay, but there's a slight adjustment that needs to be made." He paused. "The best I could do immediately is agree to be C.J.'s guardian. That means the child stays here at the ranch while the authorities search for his family."

"Oh, Dad, I didn't mean for you to take the responsibility."

"I'm not." He glanced between the two of them. "The both of you are."

It was after nine o'clock when everyone finally left and Matt put C.J. to bed. In the back bedroom with two single beds, the boy got one, and Matt got the other if he chose to take it tonight.

His thoughts turned to Alisa, and the big bed in the other room. How inviting she'd been to share it with him that weekend. How warm her trim little body was all snuggled up against his. How many times he'd brought her—

"Hey." The kid's voice got his attention. "You're going to stay here, too, aren't you?"

He nodded. "Sure. But you have to cooperate. If you give us trouble and try to run away, we won't get to stay together."

"I won't."

"And here's the other kicker. You need to go to school."

"School!"

"Yeah, like all the rest of the nine-year-old population."

C.J. turned away. For the first time, Matt saw some crack in the kid's toughness.

"What's the matter?"

No answer.

"Come on, C.J., I want to help."

"Kids made fun of me before. I got into fights."

Matt knew the feeling. "How about you meet a couple of kids who won't make fun of you? There's my niece, Gracie. She's a little older, but she'll show you around. And there's Robbie Cooper. He might be a little younger, but you'd like him. He likes baseball."

"There's Cherry Casali, too."

They both looked toward the door to see Alisa. She was wearing jeans and a fitted, rosy colored blouse that showed off her trim waist, and flare of her hips. Matt worked his throat to clear away the dryness. Damn, why this woman?

"Cherry is about your age," Alisa said.

"No girls," C.J. said.

She walked in and set down a glass of water on the table next to the bed. "In case you get thirsty." She backed away. "Good night, C.J."

"Night," he said in a muffled tone as he rolled over.

Once they were alone, Matt nudged the boy. "Hey, that's no way to act to a lady who only wants to help you."

"I don't want her help. She doesn't want me anyway."

"If that's so, why did she work so hard to get her daddy to help you? You know how important Senator Merrick is? He knows important people, and he asked them if we could take care of you."

"I didn't know that."

It suddenly hit Matt how far Alisa had gone. "Well, you do now. She's opened her home, and is trying to make you welcome. So she doesn't deserve your rude behavior."

Now that his face was clean, Matt could see the freckles across C.J.'s nose. "Okay. But do I have to go to school?"

"Hate to break this to you, buckaroo, but it's the law. All kids go to school."

"But I want to go horseback riding with you tomorrow."

"How about we see how you handle school and the way you treat a lady?" He held up a hand. "Deal?"

C.J. smacked it. "Deal." He tickled the boy until he laughed then tucked him in, said good-night and closed the door. He walked down the hall, suddenly realizing that he'd taken on the responsibility for another human being. And a child, to boot. What had possessed him to do this?

He started for the living area, but had to pass the master bedroom. The door was open and he saw Alisa sitting cross-legged on the big bed, papers spread across the wide mattress.

She looked up from her work. "C.J. asleep?"

Damn, she was beautiful. Mesmerizingly beautiful. He had trouble finding his voice. "He's down, hopefully for the night."

When she didn't move off the bed, he fought to keep those memories out of his head of the time he'd shared with her in this same bed. Damn, he didn't belong here then, or now. But that didn't stop him from walking towards her.

Those dark eyes of hers widened and he stopped. "Could I talk to you for a minute?"

She swallowed hard. So she was just as aware of him as he was of her. "What's there to talk about?"

He smiled. "The fact that we've suddenly became parents."

She fought it, but a smile appeared. "To a little boy who doesn't like girls. Any girls."

"Ah, what does a nine-year-old know?"

He caught her gaze. "That he doesn't like me."

Matt's chest tightened as he went to her. "Until he gets to know you, Alisa. Then he won't be able to resist you." Like he was having his own problem with that.

He glanced around the room for a distraction. "I like what you've done with the place." The walls had been painted blue and the hardwood floor redone and covered by a thick sand colored area rug.

"Give the credit to Sloan and Jade. They did all the remodeling."

He noticed something was missing. The tall hand-carved headboard was replaced with a spindled brass headboard. "The bed. Your great-great-grandparents' bed."

She blushed. "You remember…"

"Darlin', there wasn't much about that weekend that I could forget."

"Oh." She paused. "It's at Sloan and Jade's house. The Merricks are her ancestors, too. It's all my sister wanted from the homestead. A wedding present."

Alisa didn't know about any sister when he spent the weekend with her. Jade Hamilton arrived in Kerry Springs and announced she was the senator's daughter and the family opened their arms to her. It might have taken Alisa's half brother a little longer, but soon he fell in love.

"It's nice that everything worked out for Jade and Sloan." It was dangerous to stay on this topic. "I like the new furniture, too."

"More family heirlooms. My mother found it in the attic up at the house."

He had to get out of there, before he tried to make more memories in the new bed. "Would you mind if I camped out on the sofa and watched a little television?"

She shrugged. "Sure. *Mi casa* is *su casa.*"

Get the hell out of here, he told himself. "That's the thing, this party was supposed to be at *mi casa.* You weren't supposed to get this involved."

"I knew what I was getting into. And my dad did the best he could to keep C.J. out of the system."

"Someday the kid will appreciate that. I do."

"Right now, that little boy has a serious case of hero worship, and he thinks I'm in the way."

"I have no doubt you'll win him over." She had worked her magic on him. "Give him a little time."

"Not if he keeps blaming me for the parts of this plan he doesn't care for."

He couldn't help but smile, then he sobered to ask, "You sure you don't mind taking him to school tomorrow? I need to be at the ranch first thing."

"Not a problem. I can handle the dirty jobs."

He nodded. "Thanks. I'll pick him up at three and take him back to the restaurant."

"I should be finished at the site about four, I could come by and help with homework."

"Well, damn. Aren't we turning into a domestic couple?"

She did smile. "If this gets out, Rafferty, it could ruin your reputation."

CHAPTER SIX

SOMEWHERE around 2:00 a.m., Alisa awoke to a loud crash of thunder. She jerked up and heard the rain pounding against the window and thought about C.J. She got out of bed and walked to the back bedroom where the child slept.

She listened for voices. Hearing none, she peered inside the room to see there was only one occupant. The other bed was empty. Matt must have gone home. There was another flash and thunder soon followed. That was when she saw C.J. pull the blanket over his head. Did she go to him? Where was Matt? She glanced toward the living room, but then came another flash and a whimper. She walked to the bed and leaned over the child. "It's okay, C.J.," she soothed. "It's just thunder."

He whimpered again with the next lightning, followed by a crash of thunder. She sat down on the edge of the mattress. She brushed his shaggy hair away from his face and he didn't pull away. She continued the contact as she rubbed his back gently.

"Storms are always noisy in Texas," she whispered. "Especially out here in the open."

After a few more minutes the storm seemed to have moved out into the distance. When she heard the child's deep, even breathing she leaned forward and inhaled his soapy clean scent. She tucked the blanket around him and touched his soft cheek.

Once the door was closed she went down the hall. Since the house was small, it didn't take long for her to find her other houseguest. The dying fire in the hearth allowed her to see he was stretched out on the sofa, his stockinged feet hanging over the edge. He was sound asleep. He'd removed his shirt and was wearing a white undershirt. The top button was unfastened on his jeans.

Thunder rumbled in the background as another kind of vibration shot through her. "Oh, my," she breathed. *Just go back to bed.*

That was exactly what she'd planned to do when she heard Matt's groan. She glanced over her shoulder and saw he was moving restlessly back and forth.

Matt fought hard to stay out of hell, but he was losing the battle.

The night was pitch-black, except for the streaks of light from the rounds of artillery going off overhead. They were trapped in an ambush and he and his men were pinned on the ground, using the stranded Stryker vehicles as their only shield. Armed with only M4s, they were trying to hold off the insurgents, hoping the rest of the platoon could reach them. He wasn't even sure how many causalities, only knew he needed to get them the hell out of there. And fast.

Another round of fire, and the kid next to him dropped to the ground. Marconi was hit. Cursing, he pulled the eighteen-year-old farther back behind the ve-hicle. "Medic" he cried, knowing that he wasn't going to get a response. He worked frantically to stop Marconi from bleeding out. But there was too much blood.

Don't die on me, kid. Don't you dare! Matt cried. No! No!

"Matt! Matt, wake up!"

With a gasp, he opened his eyes and discovered that he was on the floor. He looked down to find Alisa tucked underneath him. Suddenly his body recognized the soft feminine form and quickly began to respond.

With a curse, he rolled off her. "Damn, woman, don't ever sneak up on me like that." He sat up and raised his knee, trying to slow his heart rate. Why now? Why did this happen again? And why with her?

"You cried out." She sat up and placed her hand on his arm. "Are you okay?"

He tensed, too vulnerable to let her comfort him. Not now. "I'm fine. Just a nightmare. You can say it's the price of war."

"Want to talk about it?"

The huskiness of her voice caused him to look at her. A mistake. Her dark hair was a halo around her bare shoulders. Her dark eyes were mesmerizing.

"No. Sorry, I woke you," he said.

"You didn't. The storm did and I went to check on C.J."

The kid. He'd forgotten about the kid. "How is he?"

"I stayed with him until he fell back to sleep."

"Thanks," he told her, and noticed her sleeping attire was a tank top and a pair of boxer-style shorts. He bit back a groan. "You should get back to bed, too."

She continued to watch him.

"Look, I'm not going to do anything crazy if that's what you're worried about." He raked his fingers through his hair.

"I'm not worried," she said. "I just wondered if there was anything I can do for you."

He nearly laughed out loud. "Oh, darlin', I don't think you want me to answer that one."

He watched her swallow, but his words didn't scare her off. "Who's Marconi?"

He closed his eyes momentarily. "A kid in my outfit. Look, this isn't something I want to talk about in the middle of the night. Usually if I wake up at this hour, it's not for conversation. It's for another need I want to satisfy."

He saw the flash of recognition in her eyes. He couldn't deal with the memories right now. He got to his feet, and walked across the room, away from temptation. Staring out the window, he listened to the rain run off the porch roof. It seemed the safest thing. It kept him from going back to Alisa and recreating their night together, letting her distract him from the bad dreams. He knew from memory how soft and warm her body was, how incredible her mouth was. Oh, God.

"You'd better run off to bed before we both get into trouble," he tossed over his shoulder.

Alisa ignored his warning and came across the room. "Have you talked to anyone about your nightmares?"

He tensed. He didn't need her digging into his weakness. "Not that it's any concern of yours, but yeah, I've done a whole *lot* of adjusting back into civilian life."

"Were you having a flashback the day you were thrown off your horse? It was the helicopter flying overhead that triggered it, right?"

"I was stunned, okay. Anyone would be disorientated just thrown off a horse."

"Ignoring it isn't going to make it go away."

He sent an appraising glance over her body. "You're doing a pretty good job of distracting me and making me think of more pleasant ways to spend the night."

She folded her arms over her breasts. "That's your answer to everything?"

"It's a good start." He leaned closer. Very close. When he reached for her, she momentarily resisted, but then allowed him to test the waters and his lips brushed over hers.

"Damn, woman, you are sweet." He inhaled her intoxicating scent. "I could get addicted to you," he warned right before his mouth closed over hers. He already knew how easy it would be to get lost in her.

Alisa Merrick could make all the bad memories fade away. He groaned and wrapped his arms around her back, pulling her closer against him. He angled his head and deepened the kiss. Oh, yeah, this was so much better. He stroked and tasted her until he had to break away. He couldn't do this, not like this, and not with her.

"That wasn't a good idea, Rafferty."

"You're right." He released her before he made more mistakes. "You'd better get to bed."

She watched him a moment, looking thoroughly kissed, then said, "Good night, Matt." And she walked off, leaving him standing there.

He was left grinding his teeth, hating the fact that she could see more than he wanted her to. He couldn't let that happen. He just had to figure out a way to help C.J. and keep his hands off this woman.

The next morning at 6:00 a.m., Alisa got up to start breakfast, but she found both C.J. and Matt already in the kitchen. Neither were very talkative. They were busy eating the cereal she'd picked up yesterday. She didn't need to make eye contact with the man whose kiss had nearly brought her to her knees.

Alisa left them to go take a quick shower and get dressed for work. Let him act as if nothing had happened. She had no illusions that Matt Rafferty only wanted her because she was convenient and to get her mind off asking anything more about his nightmares.

She realized she needed to let it go, too. It was his life. Their only connection was C.J.

After dressing for work, she walked to the kitchen to find C.J. waiting for her by the front door. Matt was finishing up the dishes.

"Have a nice day in school, kid," he called to C.J.

"Right," the boy murmured as he walked out and climbed into Alisa's SUV.

She sighed. "I guess I have to be the bad guy."

Even though Matt was wearing wrinkled clothes from yesterday, and had a day's growth of whiskers along his jaw, he looked good. She couldn't help but remember what had happened last night. Correction, what had almost happened. "If you'd rather, I'll take him."

She shook her head. "No, I need to get to work anyway. You'll be there to pick him up at three?" With his nod, she headed for the door, too. "I'll see you later."

He touched her arm to keep her from leaving. "Alisa, about last night—"

She didn't want to hear excuses. "You were right—it's not my business."

"No, it's not. But the kiss… Let's just say you caught me at a bad moment."

She had to work hard to hide any reaction. "Do you have a lot of those moments?"

He seemed surprised at her question. "A few, but like I said, I can handle them. Our concern is C.J. That is if this…arrangement is still okay with you. I mean, I don't want you to think that I'm going to be coming on to you while I'm staying here."

"If I thought that, I wouldn't have agreed to do it."

"Good. I should be going, too. I'll see you this afternoon."

Before she could say any more, he walked out the door before her. With a wave to C.J. he climbed into his truck and drove off.

"You'd think I'd be used to the man walking out on me." It still felt lousy.

Thirty minutes later, Alisa arrived at the Vista Verde site. She took C.J. inside the construction trailer and found her boss, Alex Casali, behind his desk. She apologized for being late and explained the situation.

"I've always said family comes first." He looked over at the boy. "Hey, C.J., you want a tour and see what Alisa does?"

C.J. glared at her. "I gotta go to school."

Alex winked at Alisa. "Class doesn't start for a while. We can spare a few minutes to show you around." He grabbed a small hard hat off the hook on the wall and placed it on the child's head. He was rewarded with a smile.

Once they were outside, Alisa took over as the project manager of Vista Verde, talking with her contractors about the pouring of the foundations on Friday. Alex stood back and allowed her to do her job. She liked that about her boss; he didn't try to take over and push his power.

A former abandoned child, Alessandro Casali was now a powerful and wealthy man in this area. A self-made millionaire. He'd started out as a rancher, and now owned a large spread outside town, the A Bar A. He had married Allison Cole, the owner of the Blind Stitch.

Alex hadn't forgotten his roots when he stepped up to help Kerry Springs with affordable housing. AC

Construction was born and Alisa was lucky enough to get the job of project manager.

"She's the boss of all of them?" C.J. asked, pointing to the crew putting together the foundation forms.

Alex nodded. "Alisa runs the entire show around here. And she's darn good at it. All the men here respect her, too." He knelt down on one knee, his voice lowered. "That's one thing you need to learn, too, son. If nothing else you always respect a lady."

C.J. gave him a stubborn look. "My daddy said women were only good for one thing."

Alex placed an arm around the boy's small shoulders. "I'm going to say your daddy's wrong on this one. I know a lot of women who are good at a lot of things. Alisa is one of the special ones. As I understand it, she called her daddy to help you so you could stay with Matt. She doesn't deserve any sass from you. Understand?"

C.J. nodded. He glanced over his shoulder and Alisa saw those big, sad brown eyes. The boy had been through so much. How much she didn't want to know.

Thirty minutes later, Alisa walked C.J. into the principal's office at Kerry Springs Elementary School. And whatever ground she'd gained earlier at the construction site had disappeared when the boy learned he had to do extra work to catch up with his class.

Alisa was beginning to think she could catch a break when it came to males in her life. She thought about Matt, but realized their main focus had to be on this child. And she had to ignore what was going on between them. Was that possible?

Could she stop reacting to Matt Rafferty? She wished.

* * *

At three Matt waited at school with the other parents to pick up C.J. When the boy appeared they walked the four blocks from downtown back to the restaurant. Once in the kitchen, he got C.J. a snack and told him to get started on his homework. He hoped that Alisa would come by soon to help the kid.

He went into the bar area and went back to nailing in the baseboards along the wall. He'd painted earlier and now could enjoy the fresh, creamy walls with the dark trim. Not too bad.

He hoped his family could pitch in to help get the dining room done before the new booths were delivered next week.

The oak bar was original, but he'd sanded it down and stained it darker. All the sports memorabilia had been removed, and a new flat-screen television took up space on the side wall. It might be a more upscale bar and restaurant, but customers would still be interested in ball games. There was a huge wine cooler installed at the far end of the bar. It was all coming together. He only hoped it was finished in time for the opening.

Suddenly his dad walked in. Sean Rafferty had always been a friendly guy with a ready smile, but since his marriage to Beth, the man had never seemed happier. His brother, Evan, was the same way after marrying Jenny. Matt liked their choices in women. Good for them. He still enjoyed the single life, or at least he had until he'd begun working two jobs.

"Hey, Dad. What brings you in?"

"Thought you might need some help." He looked around. "It's coming along. Sorry I haven't been here in a while."

"Hey, you're busy. Besides, this is my project."

"I hear you've added another job, too. Where is this young man of yours?"

"C.J.'s in the kitchen. Sorry, everything happened so fast there wasn't much time to let you know. The boy said that you and Rory let him work here."

Sean shook his head. "The story is the boy ended up in the kitchen because his old man was sitting out here at the bar. We would feed him sometimes. It wasn't like charity, Rory had him push the broom around and maybe take out a bag of trash."

"So you knew Charlie Jackson?"

His father shrugged. "The brand of beer that he drank and that he liked to talk to whoever would listen. I've seen his temper, too. So if his old man left the boy behind, it might be the best thing for him."

"Did Charlie ever talk about family or relatives?"

Sean rubbed the back of his neck. "Charlie hadn't been around long, only a few months. And he talked about Charlie, and how he was going to go work on an oil rig in the Gulf."

Matt raised an eyebrow. "You think that's where he went?"

"Not sure, but I believe that lad is better off without him."

Matt nodded, then heard his father say, "I hear that Alisa is helping you with the boy."

Again he nodded. "Just until we find some family. Then she goes her way and I go mine."

Suddenly the kitchen door swung open and Alisa came in. Matt couldn't help but stare at her. She had on a flowing black skirt that hit just below her knees, and heeled sandals showed off great legs. Her knit top was ivory and belted, accenting a slim waist and high breasts. Her hair was tied at the back of her neck, emphasizing her Hispanic heritage. She hadn't been dressed that way when she left this morning.

He managed to find his voice. "Alisa, what are you doing here?"

She blinked at him. "Helping C.J. with his math. You were busy when I came in so I didn't want to bother you." She walked up to Sean and hugged him. "Hey there, handsome."

"Hello there, pretty lass." His father kissed her and hugged her close. Why did that bother him? "How's my favorite council member-to-be?"

A bright smile lit up her already beautiful features. "I love your optimism. I was out trying to drum up some votes."

"Well, you've got mine. And we're going to help you get a lot more, too. The fundraiser is here. Remember?" He turned to Matt. "What do you say, son? You still willing to support the cause?"

"Yeah." Not that he didn't have enough to think about. "Why don't we hold it opening night?"

CHAPTER SEVEN

LATER that evening, Alisa drove C.J. back to her house, followed by Matt in his truck. She let him handle the child's nighttime routine, bath and bedtime, while she finished up her own work.

She was sitting at the kitchen table, going over the crews' schedules for the next day, when she heard C.J. say her name. She turned to see him standing in the doorway, dressed in pajamas and his hair still damp from his bath.

"Looks like you're all set for bed."

The child was starting to thrive in just the short time he'd been here. A haircut today, and some new clothes made a big difference. He still needed to put on some weight. He would, especially the way he'd been eating.

C.J. came toward her and raised those big brown eyes to meet hers. "Thanks for helping me with my homework."

"You're welcome," she said, trying to hide her surprise.

The boy was bright, and still had a little attitude toward her. She had a feeling it had something to do with his father's influence and his mother's desertion.

That seemed to be the similarity these two males shared. She couldn't know what that must have been like. People thought she had the perfect life. Yeah, right. The rich girl who'd had everything. She'd had a missing dad while he was off serving congress.

Alisa directed her attention back to the boy. "You worked hard today, too."

He shook his head. "I don't want to go to summer school. If I don't work hard now Mrs. Cooper says I hafta go."

"Then I guess we have to get you caught up."

He nodded and started to leave, but stopped. "Thanks for taking me to your work, too." He glanced away. "It was cool."

She was touched. "Well, I'm glad you think so. Maybe if we get going early tomorrow we can stop by the site again. You think you can be ready by seven?"

His eyes rounded. "Sure."

Matt called to him and C.J. turned and ran out, leaving her wondering what had caused the big change in his attitude.

Alisa put away her work. She wasn't planning to spend another evening with Matt alone. There was no way she could allow a repeat of what happened between them last night. If he was going to stay here because of C.J., fine, but she couldn't get involved with him, again.

She thought she'd escaped until he stepped into the hall from the bathroom, and they collided.

She nearly dropped her armload of papers. "Oh, sorry." She started to back away when she felt Matt's hand on her arm.

"Whoa, someone's in a hurry."

"I need to finish some work."

She wasn't about to admit the real reason. Especially when he was dressed in his signature fitted T-shirt that showed off those muscular arms and well-developed chest. God, help her. "You're probably exhausted, too. You've put in some long days."

"I never realized playing parent could be so exhausting." His blue eyes twinkled. "Have a beer with me before I head home. I want to talk to you."

Bad idea. "Sure, why not?" She dropped her papers off in her room, then followed him into the small kitchen.

He walked to the refrigerator, and took out two bottles of beer he'd brought over with some groceries. "I thought we could talk about the fundraiser." He opened them both, and handed one to her. "You still prefer to drink out of the bottle, right?" he said smiling.

He remembered that? "Yes."

Matt watched Alisa take a long drink, tilting her head back, exposing her long, slender neck. He recalled how he'd placed kiss after kiss against that soft, olive skin, causing her to shiver. How she gasped his name as he tasted every delicious inch of her.

He quickly glanced away and took a drink. Damn. He had to stop this.

"Matt, you okay?"

"Sure. My mind just wandered. The fundraiser."

She shook her head. "Look, Matt, I'm not going to hold you to your offer. Rafferty's Place opening night is special. Your family and the restaurant should be the center of attention."

"Dad and I talked about it. The Boys and Girls Club is important to the community. In fact, we're thinking this cause could bring more people in, even if it's just out of curiosity."

"It'll be more than just curiosity," she told him.

Matt leaned against the counter, trying to stay relaxed.

"There's already a lot of buzz and support about the possible reopening of the club. The ladies from the Blind Stitch are donating two quilts toward the cause. We could hold a drawing. We can throw in some of 'Rafferty's Legacy' wine, and coupons for free dinners. We might make some money."

He nodded. "We've talked about serving up some free appetizers, and a couple kegs of beer along with wine tasting, of course."

Alisa found she was getting excited over the idea. "I'm sure Jaclyn will give a donation from her ice cream store." She looked at him. "She's helping with my campaign, so I'll see what she can do about advertising the event."

"Still best friends, huh? I remember when you girls were inseparable in high school."

Alisa was shocked. They'd only been lowly freshmen when Matt was the popular senior. "You remember us back then?"

He gave his trademark grin. "Only enough to know that I'd better stay away. You were jail bait, not to mention your dad and overprotective brother."

Matt had neglected to mention that he'd been going steady with the head cheerleader, Jody Haynes. Her daddy had owned a small manufacturing company outside of town. Jody had enjoyed being the wealthy, spoiled daughter.

"You seemed to be pretty busy with your own girlfriend."

He frowned. "Ancient history."

She was curious. "You went into the army right after graduation," she said, hoping to get more information.

"That was the plan."

Then she suddenly remembered hearing that he'd lost his college scholarship.

Matt glanced away as he pushed away from the counter.

"Hey, can you think of any other people who'd be willing to donate something?"

Obviously he didn't want to talk about his past. "I'll have Jaclyn ask around. When is your grand opening?"

"In twelve days. Saturday 22. There might be a few things that won't be quite finished, but I'll have a chef, a bartender and four waitresses ready to go."

"Is there anything I can do? I mean I can wash glasses, wipe down counters, stack things."

Matt shook his head. "You're busy, too. As I recall you have a pretty big project going on with Vista Verde." He nodded toward the bedrooms. "And there's C.J."

"Helping a child is the easy part. You've done your share with him, too. But this opening is just as important."

"Speaking of which, I need to get through the Triple R's roundup this weekend."

She blinked. "How are you going to manage that?"

"With help, neighbors and a good foreman."

Matt knew he had a lot on his plate. Each one of the projects were important, but looking at Alisa right now, he didn't seem able to think about much else but her. That was the reason he needed to walk out that door. Now.

He'd be crazy to even consider trying to pick up where they left off. Trouble was he didn't seem to be listening to his own advice.

Two days later it was the Triple R Ranch roundup. It was barely daybreak as Matt left his house. The old foreman's cottage had been included in the partnership agreement with Evan. Matt ran the cattle operation. The two-bedroom had needed a little work, but for now it was perfect for just him. It gave him not only solitude after his return from overseas, but a place of his own.

Now that Evan had married Jenny and with two kids, the separate quarters gave them all privacy.

This was also the first time since Matt had gone into partnership with his brother and he wasn't sure he could pull it off, handling the ranch and opening Rafferty's Place. Thank God he had his foreman, Pete, to take up the slack.

And his family. His father would be at the restaurant today to meet with the new bartender, Kevin. Together they would stock the bar with alcohol and glassware, and Kevin would learn a few things from Sean's years of experience. Matt wanted to be there, too, but getting his cattle to market had to be his top priority right now. Even if he was short on manpower today he still needed to meet the ranch payroll.

Something else he had to worry about was C.J. He'd come to care about the kid, but it brought him right to where he didn't need to be, connected to Alisa. Now they were practically cohabitating at the one place that gave him more ideas about starting things up with her again.

Since she'd come back to town a year ago, he'd managed to stay clear of her. Now, in the past few weeks she'd been like a magnet. Worse, he hadn't minded spending that time with her.

Bad idea.

Alisa Merrick wasn't the woman for him. They came from entirely different worlds. She was seriously committed to people and causes. She needed a man to stand by her while she went out and made her mark in the world. With her name recognition, Alisa was perfect for the job. All she needed was to find the right man to help her get there. That wasn't him. Not a battle-scarred ex-soldier, a part-time cowboy who hoped to be a successful restaurant owner one day. What he wasn't good at was anything permanent like a long-term relationships.

He heard the door open and C.J. walked out. "Why can't I go with you?" the boy asked.

Matt placed his hat on his head. They'd gone over this at breakfast. "Again because it's going to be a long morning—in the saddle. You're not bad on horseback, kid, but not experienced enough for a roundup." He'd taken C.J. riding last evening since Alisa had agreed to let him spend the night here with him. He was impressed the boy could handle a horse so well.

Matt headed toward the corral and threw a quick look at the boy who was trying to keep up with him. The hat C.J. placed on his head was an old straw Stetson Matt had found in the barn. It was a little big, but it worked for the little cowboy.

"But I don't want to stay here with the girls," he whined.

Matt stopped and looked down at the boy. "Look, I told you, you can help with the branding when we get back."

The boy looked up at him. "You promise?"

He laughed. "Yeah, I promise. Unless you give Jenny and Grandma Beth trouble."

"I won't," he said and ran off toward the main house.

At the corral gate Matt met up with six other men, including his brother. Evan held out the reins to Matt's mount, Nick. The animal was already saddled and ready to go.

"Thanks," he told his brother and checked the cinch, then made a slight adjustment. "Hey, don't you have to watch your grapes grow?" he teased his brother.

"I've pretty much got them trained so they do it all by themselves. But hey, if you don't need me…"

"I think I can put up with you."

Matt heard his name and turned to see Jenny walking toward them carrying little Mick.

"I wanted to catch you before you took off," she said. "There's more help coming to ride with you."

"Who?" Matt wondered, knowing he'd called in about every favor.

She shaded her eyes and looked toward the west. "Some more neighbors." She nodded at the riders coming toward the corral on horseback.

Caught in the bright glare of the sun, he had to walk out of the corral toward the riders before he could recognize the threesome. Alisa? He glanced at the other riders, her brother, Sloan, then another rider. The senator!

They stopped in front of him. "Hey, neighbors," he called.

Sloan leaned on the saddle horn. "We heard you could use a few extra hands."

Matt was surprised to say the least. "I could. How do you feel about riding drag?"

Sloan tipped his hat back and grinned. "Sure. You and your brother have brought up the rear enough times for River's End."

Matt nodded and turned to the senator. "Thank you for coming, too, sir."

"Hell, I'm here for Sean's barbecue beef. I hear it's

on the menu." He grinned. "Louisa and Jade will be over later to help with the food."

Matt was touched. This had to be Alisa's idea. "I thought you had to work at the site today," he said to her.

She shrugged. "Alex thought I'd be more help out here."

"I don't care what brought you, I just appreciate the help."

"We're neighbors," Sloan added. "It's what we do for each other."

There had been a time when Sloan Merrick hadn't been so grateful, especially when Matt had his eye on Jade. Not too far back. Matt had wanted a chance with Jade, but the green-eyed beauty only had feelings for Sloan, and the couple married last year. She was better off with Merrick.

He glanced at Alisa, then back at her big brother's warning gaze. He didn't want him anywhere close to his sister, either. Good thing Sloan hadn't been around before.

Four hours later, Alisa was dusty and sweaty, but she felt exhilarated. She hadn't spent this much time on horseback in years.

Living in Austin she hadn't had time to go along on the River's End roundup. The Triple R Ranch's herd was small by Merrick standards, but there were still quite a few calves that needed to be branded today.

The past few days, she'd overheard Matt trying to get together a crew for today. He'd had limited time and everyone else seemed to be busy. Since the grand opening of Rafferty's Place was the following weekend, these few days were it. So Alisa asked her family for help. In Texas, it was the neighborly thing to do.

She enjoyed riding alongside her dad, allowing the foreman, Pete, Sloan and Matt to chase most of the strays. She had a feeling Sloan stayed close for other reasons. One was to find out what was going on between her and Matt.

Nothing.

They might be caring for a child together, but that was all. She and Matt had been too busy with other things to even think about starting something.

Hearing the loud hoots and hollers, she realized they were approaching the holding pens. She nudged her mother's horse, Polly, to move along to help separate the cows from the calves. The expert cow horse was good, too. She was able to help get the job done.

Once they finished, she left the bawling babies missing their mamas, and rode to the corral fence, climbed off, not surprised when her legs threatened to give out. Darn, everything hurt.

"You okay?"

She swung around to see Matt. "Yeah, it's just been a while since I've spent so much time in the saddle." Embarrassed, she put on a smile. "Where do you want me next, boss?"

With his hat tipped low over his eyes, a Western-cut shirt that hugged those wide shoulders and chest, he made one fine looking cowboy.

"Thanks to you and your family there's enough help," he said. "Why don't you go up to the house and help the ladies?"

"You don't need me because I'm a girl, or because you truly don't need me?"

He frowned. "Come on, Alisa. You're exhausted.

And I'm paying most of these guys. They can pick up the slack." He came closer and lowered his voice. "Damn, but you did good work in the saddle. I was surprised."

"Not just the spoiled, little rich girl, huh?"

His blue-eyed gaze moved over her face. "Who wouldn't want to spoil you, darlin'?"

Alisa did as Matt had suggested and went to help the ladies in the big kitchen at Evan and Jenny's farmhouse. Her mom, Beth, Jenny, Jade and even Marta, the Merrick's cook, came to help out with the food.

Long tables were set up on the patio, and loaded down with tons of food, everything from fried chicken and baked beans to Marta's famous enchiladas, and Sean's shredded beef barbecue.

The sound of cheering coming from the pen brought all the ladies out on the porch to see C.J. They walked across toward the pens. The boy held the branding iron with help from Matt, while Sloan and Evan were holding down a calf. Alisa snapped a picture just as the boy pressed the hot iron against the calf's rump and burned the Triple R brand into its hide.

It was a male rite of passage in Texas. Alisa's attention went back to Matt. She watched his long confident strides as he walked back to where the roper, Sloan, dragged in another calf. Matt easily flipped the animal on its side. A tag was attached to the ear and with a quick slice of the knife the castration was completed, too.

Matt, Evan and Sloan worked efficiently together and they seemed to be having a good time, too. The three standing side by side was an imposing picture. Similar in height, their shoulders were broad, their backs straight. No doubt about it, Matt was the best looking. He was blessed with the Irish charm. And she'd been crazy about the man since high school.

She took another picture and he looked toward her and winked. She felt the blush clear down her body. Oh, boy. She was in trouble.

"They're sure a heart-stopping sight, aren't they?"

Alisa turned around to see Jenny and close behind her was Jade.

"They're cowboys," was all Alisa would admit to. "It's hard to resist the hat and boots, and of course, the swagger."

They laughed and Jenny added, "Oh, what I like is when my cowboy takes off the hat and boots." She sighed. "What can I say?" She left it at that.

Alisa blushed. The last thing she needed was to think about Matt in the altogether.

"And you can't tell me that Matt hasn't turned your head a little."

Alisa gave a sideways glance toward her sister-in-law.

"Whatever you say I will not repeat," Jade told her. "If I hadn't been so in love with your brother, I would have been swept away by Matt's good looks and charm."

"Jade Hamilton Merrick, I'm shocked." Alisa knew how much Sloan and Jade loved each other.

"Why don't we talk about how you two look at each other? How he's been glancing over here for the past hour. I don't think he's looking for food."

Jenny's eyes widened, but she only waited to hear more.

Jade went on, "That first night at your house I could see that there was something between you two. Why do you think Sloan is so upset? He could feel the sparks, too."

"There are no sparks. There is nothing going on."

Both women laughed, and Jenny looked at Jade. "This must be the denial stage."

Alisa had to put a stop to this. "Look, if, and I mean it's a big 'if,' we were attracted to each other, we don't have the time. We have time-consuming jobs, I have the upcoming election and Matt has the restaurant. And we want different things out of life."

Jade and Jenny smiled as they looked at each other. "Denial!"

CHAPTER EIGHT

THE branding was finally finished by midafternoon and Matt and the men headed up toward the house for some food. He was hungry, all right, but mostly for Alisa. His stepmother, Beth, distracted him momentarily as she organized the crew into a line for the food tables.

That was where he caught sight of Alisa as she served up some food for C.J. and found him a place at the kids' table. Thanks to his niece, Gracie took over, making the boy welcome. C.J. didn't seem to mind at all.

Once the men had been served, Matt grabbed a plate for himself and headed toward his family who just happened to be sitting with Louisa and Clay Merrick. Soon Alisa joined the group, too.

His dad called to him. "Over here, son. We saved you a place."

He walked over and took the seat across from Alisa. He liked how she just fit in with everyone, jumped right in to do things. Okay, maybe every so often she got bent out of shape with him, but maybe he deserved it.

Clay Merrick took a big bite of his sandwich, then said, "Matt, I hope you're smart enough to put your dad's barbecue on the new menu when the restaurant opens."

"That's the one thing we wouldn't change." He

couldn't take his eyes off Alisa. "One difference is that Dad will still make it, but he won't be there as much to serve it up." He glanced at Beth, and smiled. "He's done working nights."

The senator grinned. "Well, he's earned his retirement. Right, Beth?"

Sean's bride nodded. "Let's just say we're both cutting back our hours so we can concentrate on other projects. Promoting Sean's sauce. Some travel. Going to quilt shows."

Matt enjoyed seeing his father happy. He knew he deserved this time with Beth.

Matt turned to Clay and Louisa Merrick. "You may be retired, Senator, but you sure remember how to move cattle, sir," he said. "I appreciate your help today."

"Glad I was here. That what's great about finally giving up your job. There are so many other options out there. And fringe benefits." He winked at his wife and draped an arm over her shoulders. "I can get up at dawn to help a neighbor, or stay in bed until noon."

"You couldn't stay in bed until noon if you tried," Louisa Merrick scoffed.

The senator's eyes met his wife's and he winked. "I could if I had a reason," he murmured.

It was plain to see the love between this couple. Matt couldn't help but look at Alisa, remembering when they'd stayed in bed an entire weekend. She raised her gaze to his and he felt heat rush through his body.

"I still have trouble believing you're so willing to play rancher, instead of senator," Sloan said to his dad, drawing him back into the conversation.

Clay shook his head. "It's easy. I've served my country." He glanced at his son and daughter-in-law. "Now I'm going to enjoy my family and being a grandfather."

Every eye turned toward Jade, and Sloan announced, "Yes, we're going to have a baby."

The group began to give their congratulations to the couple. Matt felt envy and he glanced across the table at Alisa. "So you're going to be an aunt."

Smiling, she nodded. "I can't wait. I'm so happy for Sloan and Jade."

Matt remembered a time when Sloan Merrick hadn't been so sure about making a commitment to Jade. Now, they seemed like one happy couple. Like his brother and Jenny, there was an intimacy shared between them, and he felt a strange surge of envy.

He shook it off. "Are the grandkids going to call you Grandpa, or Senator?"

Clay Merrick grinned. "Grandpa." He looked at Alisa. "I'm hoping in the future someone else in this family will be using the other title."

"Dad," Alisa said in a warning tone. "I'm only running for town council."

"It's not too early to start thinking down the road."

The senator's comments brought Matt back to reality. Alisa wasn't going to be staying here for long. She was a Merrick and that meant she'd be headed to Washington. It was a different world altogether than the simple life in Kerry Springs. He belonged here. And she was destined to leave. Like all the others.

The party broke up about nightfall. Alisa's brother, Sloan, had called for one of River's End ranch hands to bring a trailer to pick up the horses, and the four other Merricks rode home in Louisa's car.

Matt had offered to bring Alisa and C.J. back to her house, but he'd found the boy asleep along with the other kids in the family room. Jenny offered to keep him overnight.

Alisa wasn't sure Matt taking her home was a good idea. When he pulled his truck up in front and the sensor light came on, and she nearly jumped out and ran into the house. Her nervousness showed when she couldn't work the lock. Finally she got the door opened and stepped inside to the living room that had been lit by a small lamp beside the fireplace.

He followed her in. "I'll just get C.J. a change of clothes and be out of your hair," he said and took off toward the bedroom.

Alisa wasn't sure what caused Matt's quiet mood. Was it something she'd said or done to upset him? "I did a wash last night," she told him. "C.J.'s clean clothes are still in the laundry room."

She headed through the kitchen to the small back porch that had been insulated and converted to fit a stackable washer and dryer.

She flipped on the light. On the table were two piles of the boy's clothes.

"I thought I told you I'd do his wash," Matt said. He picked up a pair of jeans, a shirt and some underwear.

"It wasn't a problem, Matt. I was doing my laundry and I tossed his in, too."

"He's my responsibility, Alisa. You only have him because of your father."

More angry than hurt, she called him on it. "You're kidding, right? I want to help C.J. as much as you do."

Matt's blue eyes turned dark and brooding. "He's extra work for you. And with your job and the election…"

"If I didn't want C.J. here, I would have told you. I thought we'd worked out a pretty good schedule for the situation. I guess I was wrong. Lock the front door on your way out, cowboy."

She started to leave, but he grabbed her arm to stop her.

"Don't, Matt. Just leave before we say any more."

"Then maybe we shouldn't talk."

She looked up at him just as he dipped his head and brushed his mouth against hers. She froze as his lips moved over hers, taking teasing nibbles, causing her to moan in response.

She placed her hands on his chest, and her fingers curled into his shirt, holding on tight. Almost afraid to move, afraid she would break the spell.

Matt moved first. He cupped the back of her head, changed the angle of his mouth and deepened the kiss. His tongue touched her lips, and she parted for him, then he pushed inside to taste her.

He broke away. "Do you have any idea how long I've wanted to do this? All day I've been thinking about you."

A shiver trickled down her spine. "Matt." She struggled to hold it together, but she was slipping fast.

He put his hands on her waist and lifted her up on the counter, then fit himself between her legs. "Just keep saying my name like that."

"Matt," she breathed, trying to protest his action, but when he swooped down and rocked his mouth over hers, again and again, she was lost.

Alisa's hands roamed over his shirt, quickly popping the snaps, exposing his T-shirt underneath. Her hands didn't stop and tugged it up to reach underneath to feel his bare skin. She felt his shiver as her fingertips found his flat nipples.

He pulled back and looked into her eyes. "You're

driving me crazy," he groaned, then he pulled her blouse from her jeans and reached underneath with his hands.

"I want you, Alisa. That's never changed." His mouth closed over hers again in a mind-blowing kiss.

She shivered, wanting more, but knew she couldn't go down this road again. She had to stop this madness before it was too late. With her last ounce of willpower, she grabbed his wrist. "Matt. Stop."

He pulled back and looked at her. His blue eyes were dark with need and she nearly changed her mind. "I can't do this again." She tugged her blouse together.

His jaw tensed as he watched her. Only their ragged breathing filled the heavy silence, then came a ringing sound.

He cursed and pulled his phone from his jeans pocket. "Hello." He used his other hand and raked his fingers through his hair. "Hi, Jenny." He listened a moment. "It's okay. Put him on the phone. Hey, C.J. Yeah, partner, I'm coming back. I had to get some of your clothes together." He nodded. "Sure, you get to spend the night again. I'll be there in twenty minutes."

Alisa had worked swiftly to pull herself together, hoping to slow her heart rate by the time Matt hung up.

"Anything wrong?" she asked.

He left his shirt open. "C.J. got worried when he woke up and I wasn't there."

Good, then he'd leave, and she could spend the night alone figuring out how to stop wanting this man. Good luck with that. "Then you should get back."

Matt took a step closer to her. "I want to stay here with you, but you're right, the wisest decision is for me to leave."

Oh, God, help her. She held her breath until his hand dropped away, praying that he wouldn't kiss her again, but aching that he would. A man who only wanted one night, or a weekend with her. Not a future. That alone should send up a red flag, yet, she couldn't seem to resist him. "It's probably the best for both of us."

He laughed, but it was far from joyful. "If your brother and father knew what we'd just been doing, they'd kick my butt all the way to Austin."

"They'd want to kick any man I was interested in. Besides, I'm a big girl."

He reached out and ran his fingers against her cheek, he finally pulled away. "Yeah, you are. I have to go." He started out. "Thanks for letting me keep C.J. tonight."

"Sure." Although it was for the best, she didn't want him to leave. She followed him. "I can come by in the morning to get C.J. if you'd like."

He stopped at the front door. "Is it okay if I keep him for the day? I'll bring him back tomorrow evening."

She was a little jealous that she wasn't included in their time together. "He won't get under foot while you work?"

"No, he can help me with chores. And it'll give you some time for yourself."

What was she supposed to say? "Sure." She followed him outside and stood on the porch.

He stopped and looked at her. "You should have stopped me three years ago, then maybe you wouldn't hate me so much." He turned and walked to his truck.

Alisa grabbed hold of the porch pillar as he drove off down the road. "I wish I could hate you, Matt Rafferty. It would make my life a lot easier."

It was about eleven o'clock the next day when Alisa made her way to the Raffertys' ranch with C.J.'s clothes. Matt had forgotten them last night. A little apprehensive as she crossed under the arch of the Triple R Ranch and Rafferty's Vineyard. She'd been here less than twenty-four hours ago for the roundup. Would Matt take her unannounced visit the wrong way? She was only bringing by clean jeans and shirt for C.J.

With a calming sigh, she continued the drive and passed the sections of grapevines growing along the hillside lined in perfect rows. She then came to the compound and passed Jenny and Evan's two-story home. What would they think about her unannounced arrival? She could just leave the clothes with them. Or just leave.

What the heck was she doing here? Just because she couldn't stop thinking about a few hot, deep kisses that kept her up most of night. Of course she had put a halt to his advances, so she was probably the last woman he wanted to see.

Alisa was about to turn her car around when she spotted Matt coming out of the barn. She loved to watch that long easy gait as he ate up the distance. Like he had all the time in the world. She sighed. Okay she was acting like it was high school. Soon C.J. appeared and had to run to try to keep up.

Matt turned around as she parked next to his truck and rolled down her window. "Hi."

He walked to the car. "Hi. What brings you by?"

She shrugged, trying to hide her nervousness. "Huh, you forgot to take C.J.'s clean clothes with you last night." She looked at the boy. "Hi, C.J."

"Hi. Are you gonna take me back to your house?"

"No, I just brought your clean clothes."

The boy finally smiled. She handed the stack of laundry to C.J.

She turned her attention back to Matt. "Will you be going to the bar?"

After last night, Matt thought Alisa would be the last person to show up here. "No. I need to do some things here."

She nodded toward C.J. "Well you got some help?"

"Nope, he's deserting me to go off with Grandpa Sean and Gracie to see the new kid's movie in town." He turned to the boy. "Since you have clean clothes to change into why don't you go shower before your ride get here."

C.J. started to argue, but closed his mouth. "Okay. Bye, Alisa."

The boy ran off and Matt turned back to her. "He's doing better, making friends."

"That's a good thing." She nodded. "Has he told you anything more about his family?"

"Not much more than we already knew. His dad took off looking for work, and left the kid sleeping on a neighbor's sofa."

"Margie Craig," Alisa told him the neighbor's name, feeling the uneasiness between them. "How do you throw a little boy out on the street?"

"I'm thinking C.J. left on his own. Whatever, he won't talk about it. And this Margie is long gone, too."

He took off his hat as silence was only interrupted by a barking dog or a neighing sound of a horse. Then finally Matt spoke. "What about you? You're not going into work on Sunday are you?"

"Already been to the site," she admitted and he frowned. "Tomorrow I have crews working on the frames so the foundations can be poured by the middle of the week. I was heading back home, I thought I'd drop off C.J.'s clothes."

Matt leaned his forearm against the car. "Look,

Alisa. What happened last night… I was out of line. I know I took advantage."

"Like I said, I'm a big girl. It wasn't all your fault," she admitted, relieved he said something. "If it's a problem with us being together…"

He shook his head. "No, it's not. We have C.J. to consider, we need to work together for him. So you draw the line and I'll follow it."

He made it sound so easy. "Just don't overstep it."

"I think I can handle that."

"Good. Okay, I should get home."

"Why? Since you're done for the day and I lost my partner, how about rescuing this lonesome cowboy and coming on a ride with me?" He rushed on to explain. "I need to check out some down fence. It shouldn't take long."

She hesitated. "I thought we just talked about this."

"It's only a horseback ride, Alisa. And I'll be on my best behavior."

"Matt Rafferty, you wouldn't know best behavior if it came up and bit you."

"Probably true, but I'll try extra hard today," he teased.

Matt wondered why he couldn't just walk away from this woman. "How about I fix some sandwiches and we can eat along the creek? Dad's barbecue beef," he added.

Her velvet-brown eyes lit up. "You I can resist, but not your dad's barbecue." She smiled. "So lead the way, cowboy."

Thirty minutes later, with C.J. sent off with Sean to see the movie. Matt made it to the barn to find that Pete had saddled the mare, Carolina, for Alisa. He took Nick out along with a few tools to do the job. Normally he would have taken the truck, but today was too perfect to sit in a vehicle.

Matt carried the soft-sided bag and small rolled blanket and tied them onto the saddle. Together, they led the horses out of the barn and headed south. He stole a glance her way, remembering the heady, earth-moving kisses they'd shared only hours ago. Damn, she was tempting and he wanted to be with her. *Whoa, boy. Slow it down. You best remember your promise.* He shifted in the saddle and tried to concentrate on a nice easy ride.

It took another mile along the trail until they reached the downed fence. They climbed down from the horses and walked toward the tangled barbed wire.

Matt pushed back his hat. "This has old Rowdy written on it." He picked up the end of the wire.

"Rowdy?"

"My breeding bull. He likes to roam a lot. He's gone looking for the ladies."

Alisa couldn't help but think the same went for Rowdy's owner. She turned back to the split post. "Doesn't look like a one-man job."

"It never is on a ranch." Matt pulled out his cell phone. "I'll call Pete to see if we have any four-by-fours." He walked away and talked to his foreman. Alisa found she was a little disappointed she wasn't going to be able to spend some time with Matt. Not that she needed any alone time with Matt Rafferty. Not if she wanted to stay out of trouble anyway.

He walked back to her. "All set. Now let's find that shady spot for lunch."

"What about the fence?"

"I'll fix it tomorrow." He walked with her back to the horses. "Right now, I'd much rather enjoy your company, than look for an ornery bull." He grinned. "Come on. I want to show you Sunset Ridge."

It took about another ten minutes for Alisa and Matt to reach the ridge. Stopping at the top of the rise, she sat up in the saddle and looked out at the beautiful scenery. The acres of open grazing land, the unspoiled, rich green hued pastures. It was springtime, everything was in bloom. Great news for the ranches and vineyard owners in the area, the creeks were full from the recent rains. They were close to the property line between River's End and the Triple R Ranch.

Of course the Merricks had been around much longer than the Raffertys. Evan's first wife, Megan's, family had originally owned the ranch and vineyard. After her death, Evan had been the one who brought in Matt and Sean as partners to help make it a success.

Alisa looked off in the distance and could see her house. Her ancestors had come here over a hundred years ago. They'd help settle the town of Kerry Springs. A Merrick even married the daughter of the town's founder and Alisa wanted to continue that tradition by serving the town. This was her home where she wanted to make a life.

"This is a beautiful spot," she said, in awe of her surroundings.

"Yeah, I never get tied of coming here."

Alisa pointed toward the west. "You can see the homestead house from here."

"I never paid much attention before, not until I returned home." He glanced at her, recalling their weekend together. "Before that was just an old abandoned structure on the neighbor's property." He paused and shrugged. "Does it bother you that I'm so close?"

She felt a blush. Had he seen her coming and going?

"Not unless you sit up here and watch me through binoculars."

His gaze locked with hers. "Damn, woman, you're tempting enough." He sighed. "How about we find a shady spot, I'm starved." He tugged on the reins and led her to the trees. He stole a sideways glance. "Since we're being honest here, I was surprised to see you today. After last night."

There was no doubt Alisa hadn't slept, reliving Matt's kisses. How pathetic was that. "C.J. needed clothes."

He sent her his trademark grin. Pure sex. "If you say so."

He climbed down and she did the same and they walked toward the group of trees down from the ridge. She felt the breeze and saw the cool looking stream, flowing over the rocky bottom.

"Whatever the reason I'm glad. I needed someone I could play hooky with."

"Well, we both have been working pretty hard." She looked up at the tall handsome man beside her. "Especially you."

He led the horses to the creek and removed the saddlebag and blanket. "You haven't been slacking off, either." He spread it out on the ground and she sat cross-legged on the Indian print.

He sat across from her and took out the sandwiches and two cans of soda. He handed her one.

He unwrapped the large hard roll filled with barbecue beef and bit into it. With a moan of satisfaction. "Thanks to my dad, at least Rafferty's Place will have some customers. This sandwich is definitely going on the menu"

She smiled. "That's a pretty good backup plan."

Matt couldn't stop watching Alisa. Her features were

pretty near perfect, including large brown eyes he could get lost in. Flawless olive skin and a full mouth that had him feeling things for this woman he had no business feeling.

Not to get himself into trouble, Matt had to looked away. He pointed toward the pasture where several cows dotted the landscape.

"This section that borders your family's property and as far as you can see toward the east, it's mine. Of course, it's nowhere close to the size of River's End, but there are several sections. I plan to continue to run my mama and calf operation."

"It's still a good size," she stated.

He nodded. "First and foremost I'm a rancher. When I came home from the army and Evan offered me the partnership, I thought I'd died and gone to heaven." He stole another glance at her. "Raffertys had never owned anything. Growing up we had trouble even paying the rent. Not that we didn't work hard, but it sometimes seemed we couldn't catch a break." He shrugged. "Or maybe we just didn't make the right choices."

"I think your family is doing just fine now."

He felt a surge of adrenaline go through him when she smiled at him. He hated that she made him so nervous. "I'm tryin' my damnedest."

She frowned. "Why? You have nothing to prove to me, to anyone."

Wrong. He felt he had to. "Call it a man thing. Being poor makes you hungrier. You can ask my dad, Evan, even Alex Casali. We work harder to get the things we want like the Triple R. This land is my oasis, my refuge and haven. It heals me."

"Does it help with the flashbacks?"

He stiffened.

"Sorry." She reached out and touched his hand. "I shouldn't have brought it up. I'm sure you're the best on how to handle them."

He never wanted to discuss his years overseas. He only wanted to forget. "That's right, Alisa. And I can handle it." Food forgotten, he got up and walked to the stream.

Alisa knew that she'd pushed him too far. She stood and went after him. "Matt, I'm sorry. It isn't my business. I have no idea what you went through overseas, but…" She hesitated. She cared about him. She probably always would.

He turned around. He'd removed his hat and his brown hair was thick and wavy. Those blue eyes were her biggest weakness. "A lot happened, but I'm dealing with it. What I can't deal with is you being afraid to be around me."

"I wouldn't be here if I was afraid."

He held her gaze and then a glint of humor shone in those blue eyes. "With what I'm thinking right now, maybe you should be." He reached out to touch her, then pulled back. "I want you so damn much, I ache."

She swallowed the dryness in her throat, but she was still unable to speak. The breeze brushed her hair against her cheek but she yearned for his touch.

God help her. She wanted him.

Matt cocked his head. "Did you hear that?"

"What?" She listened, not knowing what he wanted her to hear.

"There it is again." He turned and looked across the creek. "It's coming from over there."

He took off and she followed as he made his way across the creek and up the rise. By then she recognized the sound of a bawling calf. Then they passed a large rock formation and found the bovine carcass. Beside the deceased heifer was her baby calf.

"Oh, Matt."

He knelt down for a closer look. "She must have had trouble giving birth." He pushed his hat back. "I knew there were a few head missing during the roundup, but that's not unusual." He looked at Alisa. "Sorry, I think our relaxing lunch is over."

She smiled, grateful that at least one of the animals survived. "Not a problem." She studied the white face doggie calf. "They're so cute at this age."

"Don't get attached," he warned.

He turned and spoke softly to the bawling calf as he went to him, then lifted him up into his arms. "Come on, little guy." He hoisted the bawling baby higher. "We'll get you something to eat."

They walked back to the horses and Alisa gathered up the blanket and the food then tied it to her saddle. Matt draped the newborn across the saddle then climbed on behind him.

He looked across at Alisa. "Don't look now, but seems we've just become parents again."

She had to push aside the longtime dream she'd had with this man, and put on a smile. "Now look who's getting attached."

CHAPTER NINE

IT WAS after six in the evening by the time Alisa headed back to her house. It had been a long day at the site, but she had to stop at the store for groceries.

When she came over the rise to her house, she was surprised to see Matt's truck already there. She didn't think they'd be back until much later, especially after rescuing the orphaned calf. Thanks to Gracie and C.J. he was named White Cloud for the marking on his face.

She couldn't help notice yesterday how natural Matt had been with the frightened newborn. When he was carrying the calf back to his horse, she'd never seen a man look so sexy. And she didn't need to think that way about him. Trouble was she knew firsthand the man's gentleness and appeal.

She walked through the door and found Matt standing at the stove stirring something in a skillet. C.J. was at the table doing his homework.

"Hey, you're back," she said as she carried the bag into the kitchen and set it on the counter. "I didn't expect you until later."

"Matt made me come back to do homework." C.J. pouted. "But I got to feed White Cloud his bottle."

Matt arched an eyebrow in her direction. "Have you eaten? I'm making Spanish rice."

"Sounds good." She had trouble looking at him without remembering them being together the past few days. She could get used to this. "And I bought dessert." Digging through the bag, she pulled out a carton from Shaffer's Ice Cream Parlor. "Does this get me out of the dishes?"

Matt smiled. "Not sure. What flavor?"

"There's Chocolate Chip and Carmel Delight."

"What do you think, kid? She's trying to bribe us with ice cream."

"If you help me with my spelling words," the child offered.

"Deal." She enjoyed the exchange with C.J. He'd changed so much in the few days since coming here. "And I'll even throw in some hot fudge topping?"

"Okay, that got me," Matt said. "I can't turn that down." He grabbed the carton, then surprised her by leaning down and placed a kiss on her cheek. "Thanks for thinking of us."

She swallowed, trying to get rid of the dryness in her throat. "Sure."

She put the groceries away, but the space in the kitchen seemed to shrink with all three of them in it. "Did you get the cattle shipped off?"

"First thing tomorrow, then I can concentrate on the restaurant. This reminds me, I have a favor to ask you."

She looked at him.

He grinned. "How do you feel about painting?"

"You mean like a picture?" She caught C.J. out of the corner of her eye. He was watching them closely.

"No, like walls. We're down to the wire at the restaurant and need to finish the main dining room before the booths are delivered on Tuesday. I'm calling in all the favors I can get. C.J. is going to help, too."

"Great. Have you ever painted before?"

The boy shook his head. "Matt's going to teach me."

"How about you, Ms. Merrick? Have you ever painted?"

"As a matter of fact, I have."

Matt arched an eyebrow. "What? Your toenails?"

That caused C.J. to collapse in a fit of laughter. She enjoyed seeing how happy the boy was these days.

Matt said, "Hey, kid, clear away your homework and go wash up. Supper's almost ready."

The boy closed his book and disappeared down the hall and into the only bathroom. Alisa turned to Matt. "It's good to see him happy."

"Yeah, as my dad would say, the lad is starting to trust us."

She smiled, then couldn't help but think about the future. "Have you thought about what you're going to do if we don't find anyone to take him?"

He frowned. "Why? Are you in a hurry to get rid of him?"

Matt's words hurt. "I wouldn't have taken C.J. in the first place if that were true. But, Matt, if he has family out there…"

"Who? A mother who deserted him?"

"We don't know if she did."

"The boy said she hasn't been around for a long time."

"He's nine years old. He might not remember why she left, or maybe they left her."

"If she's out there looking for him, she isn't trying very hard."

"Come on, Matt. You don't know that."

"And I don't want a child to get all excited that she's coming to find him."

"Is that what happened to you?" she asked. "Did your mother promise to come back for you?"

Seeing the flash of pain on Matt's face told Alisa she'd gone too far. "Matt, I'm sorry." She reached for him, but he immediately pulled away.

He shrugged, still not looking at her. "It's ancient history." He turned off the stove. "Look, I should go hurry up C.J."

Alisa refused to let him leave like this. She gripped his arm tightly. "No, please. Let me explain."

"What's to explain? It's no secret that Patty Rafferty left her husband and sons. My situation is different from C.J.'s. I had Dad and Evan."

"Doesn't matter how long ago it was. Your mother leaving was painful. You were a little boy, Matt, just like C.J. is now."

Matt remembered times when he was so scared that his dad would leave them, too.

He turned to meet Alisa's gaze, surprised to find her eyes were filled with tears. "Ah, don't," he whispered.

She blinked. "I can't help it," she said. "My dad was away a lot, and I missed him, too, but I always knew he'd come home."

He couldn't stand to see her upset and pulled her into his arms. "It's okay, Alisa. It was a long time ago."

It wasn't, though. The rejection was always there. And hadn't gotten any better when it happened years later with Jody. He swore he'd never get in that situation to feel that way again.

Then Alisa came into his life.

He'd managed to walk away once, but now, holding her made him realize how dangerous she was to his heart. And he had to resist the temptation.

He released her. "Don't worry, Alisa, I get plenty of

attention from women. So I don't need you to be moth-
ered."

She stiffened. "Sorry, I won't get carried away."

He met her gaze again. "And that's the last thing we
need. Right?"

She quickly composed herself and nodded. "So back
to C.J.," she began. "Matt, think about this. What if
Charlie was the one who ran off with the boy?"

"You mean C.J.'s father kidnapped him from the
mother?"

She nodded. "It happens. A bad divorce. A bitter custody fight. There could be a number of reasons why his
mother wasn't in his life."

"Okay, think about this. What if the father had a
good reason to take the boy?"

She nodded. "Okay, but then if C.J. meant so much
to Charlie, why did he take off and leave the boy behind?"

Matt couldn't answer that.

Alisa continued on, "I'm sure the sheriff is doing
the best he can to find his family, but we need to help
more."

He glared at her. "Are you going to pull some more
strings?"

"Hey, it was those strings that kept C.J. out of the
system."

Matt didn't want any more help from Alisa. Their
lives were too entangled as it was. Yet, he had to think
about the boy. Matt had been spread thin enough with
trying to handle two jobs. When the restaurant opened
he would have to work nights for a while. C.J. deserved
more.

He glanced at Alisa. She was incredibly beautiful and
he had to find a way to get her out of his life before he

got in any deeper. Maybe finding a responsible parent for C.J. would help.

"Okay, call in the Merrick big guns."

The next morning, Alisa had gotten C.J. ready for school, alone, because Matt had to load the cattle for transport back at his ranch. They'd both missed not seeing him at breakfast, but she'd distracted the child by telling him they could go by the construction site before school. That was the incentive the boy needed to get moving.

At noon she had a quick lunch with her father and a private investigator. The senator had already hired someone to do the preliminary work on C.J.'s case.

Late that afternoon, she'd finished her workday and was headed to the restaurant with her surprise, wondering how Matt would feel about it. As Alisa walked inside she heard the sound of laughter. She and P.I. Rick Lawton headed past the bar area to the main dining room. That was where they found Sean, Evan, Matt and C.J. loaded with rollers and brushes, painting the walls and wood trim.

She felt a sudden jolt of jealousy wanting to share the moment, too. She shook away the feelings, recalling that a few kisses didn't mean anything to Matt Rafferty. It was time for both of them to move on. So the quicker this got settled the better.

"Is that the boy?" Rick asked.

"Yes. He's happy whenever he's with Matt. In fact, he's with all the Raffertys."

"He's a lucky kid to end up in a good situation."

Alisa glanced over her shoulder at the man in his early forties. Big and fit, Rick Lawton wasn't bad looking. He was a retired police officer from Dallas who'd gone into private investigating. He'd talked to the sheriff already and got C.J.'s background.

"Well, just don't let C.J. fool you. He's a streetwise kid. He doesn't trust many people, especially women."

Rick smiled. "I bet you won him over."

"I wish it was that easy. He's a tough sell."

Rick sighed. "If his mother ran out on him, I can't blame him. Let's see what else I can learn."

Alisa agreed and together they walked into the dining room. "Hey, it doesn't look like you guys need my help."

Matt turned around with a smile, but it quickly died when he saw her companion. Sean came over to greet her, so did Evan. "Lass, it's good to see you anytime," the older Rafferty said.

"Thank you, Sean." She smiled. "Sean, I'd like you to meet a friend of my father's. Rick Lawton, this is Sean Rafferty, and his sons, Evan and Matt, and this is C.J."

"Nice to meet you all."

"How do you know the senator?" Sean asked.

"I've done some work for him over the years." He looked at the child. "What do the letters C.J. stand for?"

The boy frowned, but answered, "Just C.J."

"I bet you all are ready for a break," Alisa said. "Why don't I get us some drinks?" She headed back to the kitchen, not surprised to find that Matt followed her.

"Who is that guy, really?"

She looked over her shoulder as she opened the large refrigerator. "Exactly who he said he was. He did work for my father. He's a private investigator."

"Damn. How did you get him so fast?" He raised a hand. "You've already started the search, haven't you?"

She shook her head. "No. I only contacted my dad

this morning and learned he had started his own search. But isn't it better this way?"

"Not if C.J. is put through the third degree again."

"Rick's a professional, he can handle it discretely."

"Well, *Rick* better, because C.J. is a pretty savvy kid."

Why was Matt so angry with her? "I know, I've already warned him."

"Like that's going to help."

"I bet he gets some information."

"You have a lot of faith in your Rick guy."

"He's not my Rick anything," she argued. "Just have faith that my dad hired the best."

Matt didn't respond.

"What? No comment?"

He gave her that signature Rafferty grin. "I'll let you know later." He picked up some of the drinks, and Alisa had no choice but to follow him. The man infuriated her. It was a good thing their time together was coming to an end. She needed to move on with her life.

Two hours later, they'd finished painting, and after cleaning up Evan offered to take C.J. home for supper with the family. Since the boy's homework was completed, he was allowed to go, but had to be back at Alisa's by nine. That gave the boy time to look in on the calf after supper. That way, Rick could continue looking for clues in the boy's past.

Alisa parked by her front door, Matt pulled in beside her, then the investigator arrived in his vehicle. Rick was going to go through C.J.'s personal things. She wasn't sure it was fair to invade the child's privacy. The only thing that made her okay with it was the fact that his mother could be out there, hurting over her son's disappearance.

And they only thing that C.J. had admitted to was the town he came from was the name of a song. The one the child had showed the most reaction to was "Amarillo by Morning."

Rick walked into C.J.'s bedroom as both Alisa and Matt stood in the doorway and watched as the investigator expertly moved around the space. Everything he'd touched he put back exactly where it came from. He checked under the mattress, under the bed, in the corners of the closet. That was where he found the shoe box.

Rick placed the box on the bed and removed the lid. Inside there weren't shoes but a little boy's treasures. Some cheap plastic army soldiers along with some other worthless trinkets.

It made her sad what little there was. They had bought him a few things, but C.J. never seemed to want much.

On the bottom of the box was a folded picture.

Rick took it out and opened the creased photo. "Bingo." Matt and Alisa came closer and looked down at the picture of C.J. and a small blonde woman dressed in a waitress uniform. They were standing in front of a building, the Cottage Restaurant.

"C.J.'s mother?"

Rick turned the photo over and read, "Loretta Pruett. First day on the job." He read the date. "That was six months ago."

"That doesn't mean she's been looking for him," Matt added.

"They look pretty tight," Rick said. "And seeing the condition of this picture, the boy has kept this pretty close." He took out a camera, and snapped a picture of the photo. Then he put everything back exactly like it was and returned the box to its place in the closet.

"What are you going to do now?"

"I'm going to Amarillo and this restaurant. Hopefully I'll find Loretta Pruett. I have a feeling I'll learn why Ms. Loretta hasn't gone to the police." He shook his head. "I'm betting my reputation that good old Charlie has been lying to his son."

"What do we do?" Alisa asked.

"Exactly what you have been doing, take care of C.J."

They walked Rick outside. "I'll call you as soon as I get some more information."

They stood on the porch and watched as he drove off.

Matt was having trouble understanding any of this. What if C.J.'s mother hadn't abandoned her son? All this time…

"What do you think?" Alisa asked.

"I don't know. I'm only concerned about C.J."

"It would be wonderful if he could be with his mother again."

"Only if she checks out," he added. "Remember she apparently didn't call the police since C.J. disappeared."

"Maybe she was afraid. If her husband was abusive, and Charlie convinced her that the only way she'd ever see C.J. again was to do what he said."

He sat down on the railing and faced her. "Damn. Charlie has really done a number on the kid." His gaze met hers. "Okay, let's leave it to the experts to handle this."

She placed her hand on his arm. "Matt, I know this is tough. C.J. could be leaving soon."

It was hard not to react to her touch. He liked being

around Alisa all the time and C.J. had become more than a daily routine.

"Not until everything checks out," he warned. "What about you, Alisa? You ready to get your house back if and when they locate C.J.'s family?"

She blinked and he could see the tears welling up. She straightened. "Sure. Who needs a nine-year-old under foot? Not to mention he's wrecked my booming social life."

He smiled. "Not to mention your booming political life."

She grinned at that, and he'd never seen anything so beautiful. "Your life is pretty busy, too, Mr. Entrepreneur."

He sobered. "I guess we both are. But I think we did pretty good at being stand-in parents," he said, knowing any more time with Alisa Merrick could have him thinking about more, much more.

No. Their reason for being together was quickly coming to an end. And he knew it was going to be one of the hardest things he'd ever had to face.

It was two days later on Friday afternoon. The weekend couldn't come fast enough for Alisa. Yet when she came out of the construction trailer and saw Gladys Peters she nearly turned around and went back inside.

The sixty-five-year-old woman had gray hair that was cut short in a manageable style. Her stocky build and nondescript clothes were kind of like her personality.

"Alisa."

"Hello, Gladys. What brings you out this way?"

"We need to talk."

"Okay. What's on your mind?" As if she didn't know.

"It's this crazy idea of yours to reopen the Boys and Girls Club. You're never going to raise enough money to remodel that place. The building should be torn down."

"Why? The structure is sound."

"It's an eyesore. The council feels it's a bad investment to throw money into it when it will be a drain on the town's budget."

"That's why I'm going to raise a lot of money. And there's other money out there, too, federal, state. Dad's looking into funding."

Gladys smiled, but not happily. "Just because you're a Merrick doesn't give you the right to march in and decide what's good for this town."

"It's a vacant building." Alisa paused. "Unless you already have someone who wants to move into that area?"

"I'm not discussing council business."

"Why not? The meetings are open to the public."

"You'll never be able to pull this project off on your own. For one thing, construction costs are too high. And the council will never approve the money to help run the place even if the doors open. As a member, I'll see to it that it never happens."

Alisa had to smile. "You're taking a lot for granted, since you haven't won the election yet."

She made a snorting sound. "I've been a trusted member of the council for years. The townspeople know they can count on me. You're young and too inexperienced."

Did other people think that, too? "I don't agree, Gladys. Remember, everyone has a vote. So don't forget about the small shop owners, and the lower income citizens in this town, especially the kids who need a place to go in the summer and after school. It's time those people have a say where their tax dollars go."

The woman shook her head. "Well, they aren't going to get this property, not if it gets sold."

Alisa was about to vent her anger, then she heard her name called.

She turned around to see Matt and C.J. coming toward her. "Matt, what are you doing here?"

Eyeing Gladys closely, Matt stepped up beside her. "C.J. has something to tell you."

The boy grinned. "Alisa, I got all my spelling words right on the big test."

"Oh, C.J.! That's wonderful."

Matt rested his hand on the child's shoulders. "We thought you might like to go out to dinner with us to celebrate."

They were including her? "I'd love to go."

C.J. seemed pleased by her acceptance, but Matt's smile faded as he turned to Gladys. "Hello, Mrs. Peters. I hope we're not interrupting anything."

"Just me trying to convince Alisa to give up on her unrealistic endeavors." She looked from Alisa, to C.J. then back at Matt. "Maybe you can persuade her to give up on lost causes."

Matt took a step closer and slipped his arm around Alisa. "That's what makes her so endearing. She cares about people."

Gladys looked smug. "Well, looks like you have a lot of friends in your corner. Too bad they aren't influential."

"I don't know about that."

Alisa caught Alex Casali walking toward them.

"Hey, Mr. C.," C.J. called. "I got a hundred percent on my spelling test."

"All right!" They exchanged high-fives, then Alex turned his attention to the adults.

"Alisa, I forgot to mention something to you earlier. The bid I gave you for the Boys and Girls Club, all the labor and materials will be waived by AC Construction. All the subs agreed to work for minimum cost."

"Oh, Alex," she gasped. "That's so generous of you."

"I figure it's better for everyone in this town. And you can expect Allison and me at the fundraiser. We still need new equipment, too."

Alex then smiled at Gladys. "I hope you're ready for a fight, Ms. Peters, because this candidate stands for change."

Matt spoke up. "And we stand behind her."

CHAPTER TEN

SATURDAY night had arrived along with the much anticipated opening of Rafferty's Place. Matt's new chef, Luke Quincy, was in the kitchen finishing up the appetizers, hopefully to a standing room only crowd.

Kevin was behind the bar checking the supply of glasses. The kegs were tapped and ready. Three experienced waitresses and a busboy were ready, too. All they needed were customers.

Matt walked past the bar and into the new dining room. The walls were painted eggplant with dark stained wainscoting. New black booths lined the walls, and over each table hung a small chandelier, making each space more intimate. Not too over the top, he hoped. Just enough class for Kerry Springs.

"It looks wonderful!"

He turned to see Beth holding a centerpiece of fresh cut flowers. "You think so?"

"Oh, Matt." She placed the bouquet on a table. "You did a wonderful job of remodeling this place. The colors are wonderful. So rich."

Jade picked them. "We're hoping people will like the changes, too. After all, Rory's was practically a landmark."

"Well, this town can stand a little dressing up." She

ran a glance over him. He had donned charcoal trousers and a buttoned down collared light blue shirt, no tie.

"You look mighty handsome, son," she said.

"Thank you." He glanced over her shoulder and saw Alisa come through the door.

Oh, boy. She looked gorgeous. In black, wide leg trousers and a cream colored silk blouse with a chain belt hanging low at her trim waist. Her coal-black hair hung down in an angular cut against her cheeks.

Carrying a large glass fish bowl to the table where all the prizes were displayed, she set it down and smiled as friends and family started filing in. She finally looked in his direction and waved, then walked over.

"Oh, Matt, everything looks so wonderful." She released a breath. "Everyone I talked to is so excited about tonight. I think you can expect a full house."

"It's what I hoped for."

She locked those incredible bedroom eyes on him. "You did more than hope, Matt, you worked hard for this." She smiled. "I'm so happy for you. This has got to feel like a dream come true."

"Almost. Wait here." He went to the bar and grabbed two glasses, then poured champagne into them. He returned to her. "Before the night gets too crazy I want to start it off right."

She blinked. "Okay."

He raised his flute. "To dreams coming true."

"For all of us," she added.

They took a drink, then he leaned down and brushed a kiss across her surprised mouth. The past couple of weeks, he'd behaved himself. Maybe tonight he was feeling he wanted more.

"What was that for?" she asked.

"For a lot of reasons, but mostly because it's hard for me to resist you."

She swallowed and then quickly recovered. "Let's hope the voters feel the same way. However it turns out, Matt. I can't thank you enough for helping with this fundraiser."

"I guess we were a big help to each other."

Matt took another sip, but his gaze never left Alisa's face. "No doubt you're going to raise a lot of money."

"It doesn't hurt to have a good-looking Rafferty in your corner, either. I bet you could charm some money from the female patrons."

His lips twitched. "So what do we do, divide and conquer?"

The noise level grew as people began to drift in. He moved closer and took Alisa's hand. "You know what I wish?"

She shook her head and he inhaled her soft scent.

"I wish everything good to happen for you. I meant it, I want all your dreams to come true."

Again, she looked surprised. "Back at you, too."

"So how about later?" he continued, knowing he should walk away, but he couldn't do it. "After the night is ended and everyone has gone, we meet in the kitchen? For our own celebration."

She hesitated, then finally nodded. He reluctantly released her hand and they both went to make tonight a success.

Two hours later Rafferty's Place's Grand Opening was going strong. The bar was packed with people. In the dining room, the booths were filled and orders taken with paying customers sampling their new menu.

Matt was pleased to hear raves about the food and

the Rafferty Vineyard wine. Of course there were some people who came in just out of curiosity, wanting to get a look at the new place, and get the free appetizers and beer.

He at least pushed them to buy a dollar raffle ticket.

Oh, yeah, so far the night was going well. He couldn't have dreamed that it would be this successful. Smiling, he watched people mingle. Most of them were from here in town, but there were many who were strangers. Hopefully not for long.

Pulling double duty, he went behind the bar. Grabbing two beer mugs, he filled them from the tap and set them on the bar for customers. His father also helped out serving drinks. He eyed Kevin as he moved effortlessly in the narrow space. There was standing room only, divided up almost equally between men and women who came to enjoy the evening. He was impressed by how well his new bartender worked under the busy conditions, not to mention all the attention he got from the female patrons.

A few subtle propositions were tossed in Matt's direction, too. It felt strange, making him wonder why he wasn't that interested in attention from the pretty women of Kerry Springs. He glanced across the room toward Alisa. She was standing by the door, greeting the people coming in.

Although it was his grand opening, he felt more comfortable behind the bar. He'd make the money for Rafferty's Place serving drinks, and Alisa could get donations for the Club as they walked through the door. A win-win situation for both of them. It was both their nights, and they did better working separately.

Matt had tried the couple thing. Most women had

thought he was better on the dance floor, or the bedroom, than to bring home to the parents.

He quickly cleared away some glasses and gave the counter a swipe. He stole another glance at her as she turned toward him. Those velvet-brown eyes locked with his. She smiled and his heart began to pound hard.

Damn. Since the moment they'd met she'd had this effect on him. He released a breath. He knew he'd be lying if he denied he had feelings for Alisa. Problem was what was he going to do about it?

Kevin came up beside him and gave a low whistle. "Hey, boss, looks like you're getting some high class clientele tonight."

Matt looked up to see Alisa greeting her father, her mother, Louisa and brother, Sloan and his wife, Jade, and then there were two more men.

"Who are you talking about? The senator?"

"Well, him, too." Kevin nodded toward the men shaking Alisa's hand. "If I'm not mistaken those two gentlemen are State Representatives. I'm not sure of their names. I can find out, though."

Matt shook his head, eyeing the older men. "I'm sure Alisa will introduce us."

As if on cue, Alisa walked the group toward the bar. Matt put on a smile and met them at the open end of the counter.

"Matt Rafferty I'd like you to meet Joe Kelley and Michael McClure. Gentlemen, this is our host tonight, Matt Rafferty."

Matt shook their hands. "Glad you could make it."

"We're glad to be here," McClure said. "The senator has been raving about this place for weeks. And we wanted to show our support for Alisa's cause."

Matt smiled. "The Boys and Girls Club means a lot

to all of us," he added, pretty sure they were looking at Alisa as a future political candidate. "Let me get you something to drink. We have beer on tap, and of course, Rafferty Vineyard wines."

They all agreed on the wine. Matt returned with four glasses filled with last year's vintage of Chardonnay.

The gentlemen wandered off, but Alisa lingered as Matt handed her a glass. She took a sip. "I shouldn't drink. I need to keep a clear head."

He stood close to her, stealing a private moment before they both had to go back to work. "You've earned it."

She smiled and took another sip, then handed it back to him. "Save it for me...later." She turned and left.

His heart sped up again as he watched her walk away. She went back to greeting people.

"She might breathe some fresh air into this town, but don't be fooled by her sweet-talkin' ways."

Matt looked at the middle-aged man sitting at the end stool. Kurt Harper had been a regular customer at Rory's. He never had a problem giving his opinion. "Say what you mean, Harper."

"Don't take offense, Rafferty. I'm only tellin' you that little lady isn't long for Kerry Springs. She's a Merrick. Just like her daddy and granddaddy, she'll be off to Washington like that." He snapped is fingers. "She'll probably marry one of those pantywaist congressmen. Damn waste if you ask me."

Matt kept his expression unchanged, but he knew what Kurt was saying was true. How long would Alisa really be around? While he was working to put down roots, she was probably dreaming someday about taking off back to Austin, or D.C.. She was out to save the world, and he'd be right here at the neighborhood bar.

"Hey, Matt."

He looked up to see Jaclyn hop up on one of the empty stools. "Great party."

"Yeah, it is."

"I have a favor to ask you."

He waited.

"I was wondering if you could be bought."

"What's on your mind?"

"How about giving the ladies what they want?"

Alisa was having a good time, but she could use a moment to catch her breath. The evening had been going fine. Also most perfect, in fact. The one glaring problem had been her father. Clay Merrick was pushing her. He said he wouldn't but bringing in the big guns from Austin only showed her that he wanted more for his daughter than a seat on Kerry Springs' town council.

Question was, did she want more? Merrick had always been involved in politics; it went back generations. And since she was the last of the Merricks, it was expected. Being daddy's girl, she wanted to please him.

Alisa turned her attention toward the bar to see Matt. Funny thing was she wanted to be Matt's girl.

She joined Jaclyn at the donation table. The silent auction was still going on for the quilts and a few of the more expensive items, which included a weekend trip to Las Vegas. Thanks to Jaclyn, who was smarter than Alisa gave her credit for, who'd put the items up online to get bids.

Her campaign manager glanced around the crowded bar area. "This turnout is better than I hoped for."

"Most are here more for the free stuff," Alisa reminded her. "Remember this is Matt's grand opening." And she hoped that they'd all return as regulars. After hearing the glowing reports about the food she didn't doubt it. She wanted this to be a successful night for him, too.

"They came to see you, too," Jaclyn assured her. "And if Gladys tracked you down yesterday that means she's worried about you." Her friend grinned. "I love it."

Alisa had trouble thinking about the election right now. She was too distracted by Matt. They were supposed to meet later. Was she willing to take this further with a man who hadn't wanted her in the past? She glanced toward the crowded bar. A lot of the men were friends of his and the girls were probably hoping Matt would give them some attention. He wasn't disappointing them, either.

"You ready?" Jaclyn asked. "I got a few surprises, especially from one hunky bar owner."

Alisa gripped her arm. "What did you get Matt to do?"

Jaclyn studied her. "Does it matter? You said you two aren't a couple. Has something happened that you haven't told me about?"

There'd been a lot she hadn't even admitted to herself. The one big fact was she hadn't stop loving Matt Rafferty. But Matt hadn't admitted anything, either. Was that the reason he wanted to meet later?

"Alisa. Has something happened between the two of you?"

She shook her head. "Of course not."

"Okay then." Jaclyn picked up the microphone and called for people's attention.

"First of all, Alisa and I would like to thank you all for coming tonight. And secondly, thanks to Matt

Rafferty for allowing us to use his grand opening to support this cause. Thank you, Matt."

Cheers went up as he waved from behind the bar.

"Now, I'd like to introduce the woman of the hour, Alisa Merrick, Kerry Springs' candidate for town council."

More cheers as Jaclyn handed the mike over to her. Alisa smiled and began to speak. "I can't tell you how pleased I am that you all came out tonight in support of the Boys and Girls Club, and for your generosity. And a big thanks to AC Construction for the gift of doing the repairs on the building. Thank you, Alex and Allison." Another round of applause. "I'm sure the town council will have to take this matter seriously."

"It will when you're on the council," someone called out.

Everyone cheered and she smiled. "Thank you again for coming tonight."

Alisa then handed the mike back to Jaclyn who announced the winners of the silent auction and the next ten minutes they drew more names from the fishbowl.

"Okay," Jaclyn went on. "That's the end of the drawing, but I got a last-minute prize." She smiled. "It's dinner for two, right here at Rafferty's Place. So what am I bid for Chef Luke's specialty and for his decadent red velvet cake?"

There was a long silence, then Jaclyn said, "Not enough to entice you?" She grinned. "How about if Matt Rafferty is your dinner companion?"

Alisa bit back a gasp.

"Two hundred dollars," a woman called out.

"Two-fifty."

"Three hundred."

Alisa felt an odd sensation. Matt had agreed to this?

She glanced toward the bar, but Matt wasn't looking her way. He was busy joking with the guys. By the time the bidding stopped, an evening with the man she'd fallen in love with was worth three hundred and fifty dollars.

Is that what a broken heart went for?

The evening finally ended around midnight. Matt was exhausted, but was too busy with cleanup to stop. He wanted to catch Alisa but she was always occupied in conversation. He'd hoped he could have gotten the chance to explain about the auction earlier, but he couldn't get to her.

Finally the kitchen was closed and cleaning was in full swing with his crew, so Matt went to find Alisa. Her parents had left, too. Maybe she'd walked them out. He said goodbye to his family. Since C.J. was spending the night with a friend, Robbie Cooper, he'd didn't have to worry about the boy until the morning.

That gave him time to be with Alisa. If he could find her. He checked on Kevin and the waitresses who'd finished clearing the tables in the dining room and were busy splitting up their evening's tips. He told them to go home.

Jaclyn called to him. "I'm going to leave now. Is there anything else you need?"

"Yeah, where's Alisa?"

She blinked. "She left about an hour ago. I thought she'd said goodbye to you."

Okay that hurt. "No. I guess we missed each other. Did she go back to the ranch?"

Jaclyn shook her head. "No. She's staying in town at the condo."

"What's her address?"

She hesitated.

"Come on, Jaclyn. I thought you ran this auction idea by Alisa?"

"Well, sort of," she said. "How was I to know that it would bother her? She said you weren't a couple."

Matt wasn't happy about that. "Then I need to set her straight about some things."

She gave him directions. "Just be sure you're going there for the right reasons. Don't hurt her again, Matt."

"It seems I've already accomplished that. Now, I'm going to try to fix it."

Twenty minutes later, Matt was wondering the same thing. Maybe he should just drive home. He wanted Alisa like no other woman before, but this could end up a mess, for both of them. Still after making the night deposit at the bank, he pulled into the town house complex. He managed to find her unit and knocked before he could change his mind.

He saw the peephole and felt Alisa's eyes on him. "It's late, Matt. Can we talk another time?"

"Come on, Alisa. I need to talk to you now. I'm not leaving, either, so unless you want me to wake up your neighbors, you best let me in."

The door opened and she allowed him into the small entry, but he walked into the main living area. It was dim with only a light from the kitchen.

She marched after him, dressed in a tank top and boxer style shorts. "Why are you here, Matt? It's nearly one o'clock in the morning."

"I thought we had plans to meet when the party was over. Why did you leave?"

She shrugged her narrow shoulders. "You seemed to be occupied with your pretty dinner companion."

Well, damn. She was jealous. "Look, that wasn't my idea. Jaclyn talked me into helping the cause. I only went along with it to raise money." He went to her. "It's only a dinner, Alisa."

Alisa shook her head. She had no right to be this way. "It's not any of my business. Look, Matt, this was a bad idea. We both know what happened the last time."

He nodded, and knew he could recite a dozen more reasons. Yet the last thing he wanted was for her to close the door in his face. "So tell me, Alisa, why can't I just leave? Why can't I go to sleep at night without you on my mind? Without wanting you? Why do you think I've stayed away from you for the past few years?"

She froze. He cared about her. "Because you didn't like me?"

He grinned and her heart tripped. "It sure as hell would make things easier if that were true." His gaze locked on hers. "But if you tell me to leave, I will. And never bother you again."

She couldn't manage a breath let alone form words. Finally she was able to speak. "I don't want you to go."

He eliminated the space between them and cupped her face in his hands. "I'm glad." Then he bent down and kissed her. It was so brief that she whimpered when he pulled away, but his mouth was soon back on hers. He drew her close as he deepened the kiss, changing the angle for better access. Soon his tongue brushed against her lips and she opened willingly, hungry for him.

He broke off, but rained kisses along her jaw to her ear. "I want you, Alisa Merrick."

"Oh, Matt." She was afraid. This man had the power to hurt her. He had once and could again, but desire overruled any doubt.

His mouth captured hers again, weakening her resolve, which wasn't hard to do. She was hanging on by a thread when his hand slipped under her shirt. She shivered as his fingertips skimmed over her bare flesh until he cupped her breasts.

"God, Alisa." He pressed against her body, letting her feel his desire for her. "I've never wanted another woman the way I want you."

"I want you, too, Matt." She gasped as his fingers caressed her nipples, causing them to harden. "Make love to me."

He lifted her into his arms. "Show me the way. Fast."

She pointed down the hall. "The second door on the left."

He carried her into the master bedroom with a king-size bed. The covers were already pulled back. He lowered her down on the mattress. "It's an awful big bed to sleep in alone."

"Sleeping isn't on my mind right now."

She felt his grin against her cheek. "That's my girl."

She closed her eyes and pretended that was true as Matt began to take her to heaven.

CHAPTER ELEVEN

ALISA was jerked awake by the sound of Matt's voice. She raised her head to see him in the middle of the big bed, moving restlessly against the tangled sheets.

"No! No! Stay back," he cried out.

She sat up, knowing enough not to get too close when he was having one of his nightmares. She called his name, "Matt." Then a little louder. "Matt."

He gasped and opened his eyes as he tried to sit up. She coaxed him to lie back down with soothing words. She then leaned over and kissed him, moving closer as she wrapped her arms around him.

"Shh, it's okay, I'm here," she whispered.

She held Matt tight, stroking him and soon he started to relax and only then did she know she could, too.

Matt felt Alisa's soft body against him, her arm across his chest. Her hushed words against his ear. He pulled her closer.

She raised her head in the darkness, only the moonlight coming through the open window outlined her face. "Are you okay?"

He nodded, feeling far too vulnerable.

"You want to talk about it?"

He hated that she saw his weakness. "Not sure I can."

She just plowed ahead. "Did you lose a lot of men overseas?"

"More than I want to think about," he admitted. "Some were too young to even be there. They hadn't even begun their lives yet. Yet so cocky and they felt invincible, that nothing bad could happen them. Dammit, but it did."

"Marconi?"

Matt swallowed hard. "Carlos was the worst. For months I tried drill some sense into head." His voice grew husky. "I couldn't keep protecting him. When we were ambushed that night, once again he tried to play hero. I called to him and called to him to stop." He felt the sting of tears. "He just kept on going, gun blazing."

"It wasn't your fault, Matt." He heard the tears in her voice. "You can't take care of all of them."

"That didn't make it any easier when I visited his parents. I thought they'd be angry at me because I was his sergeant and I should have kept their son safe." He looked at her. "You know what they told me?"

She shook her head.

"They said they were happy to meet the man their son wrote about. They said that I was Carlos's hero."

She smiled. "Why is that so hard for you to believe?"

"The men and women who gave their lives are the heroes. I'm just one of the lucky ones who managed to make it home."

"And I'm glad you did." She laid her head on his chest.

Matt stared out the window at the moonlight. He should feel good with Alisa beside him. But it quickly died when dread washed over him. He'd spilled his guts to her. Could he live up to her expectations? He'd let people down; his mother and Jody.

How soon before she left him, too?

The next morning came too soon as bright sunlight flooded the bedroom. Alisa rolled over and found the other side of the bed empty. Matt. She jerked up and was relieved to see him standing across the room already dressed. She smiled. "Good morning."

"Morning," he replied.

She sat up and brushed her hair back. "You're up early."

"I need to get back to the ranch."

"Oh." She glanced at the clock, seeing it was after seven. "I guess someone has to feed the cows. Want some help?"

"No, you can go back to sleep. I just didn't want to leave without telling you."

Something felt wrong. Grabbing the sheet and wrapping it around her naked body she stood and went to him. "Sure I can't convince you to take the morning off?" She rose up on her toes and kissed his jaw. "Unless you're tired of me already?"

"Hardly." Matt knew that would never happen with her. A familiar tightness in his chest brought up old wounds and memories of the times he'd reached out, but happiness would elude him. Could he let Alisa in and chance it happening again?

She smiled and a funny sensation tightened his chest.

Oh, yeah, he could get used to her.

"Show me, Matt," she challenged. "Like you did last night."

God, he was tempted and his cell phone went off. He reached into his pocket. "Hello."

"Matt, it's Rick Lawton. I couldn't get any answer from Alisa's phone."

Matt froze. Why was he calling so early? "She's right here."

He started to hand her the phone when the P.I. said to him, "You can take this, Matt. I wanted to let you know I've located Loretta Pruett, and I'm bringing her to Kerry Springs. We'll be there in about two hours."

"Whoa. What do mean? You can't—"

"Look, Matt, it's going to be okay. It's what we thought, Charlie took their son without permission. She's been trying to get Caden back. That's C.J.'s name. Caden. Just meet us at the sheriff's office in about two hours."

"What about C.J.? He won't want to see her."

"We all agree it's not a good idea to spring her on him yet. So we all need to meet at the sheriff's office and discuss what to do."

Matt wasn't sure about this. He was going to get some answers before he turned the boy over anyone.

"We'll be there." He hung up and looked at Alisa. "It seems Loretta Pruett has decided she wants to be a mom again."

Two hours later, Alisa had showered and dressed while Matt had gone back to the ranch to help with chores and change clothes. After talking with her father, she drove herself to the sheriff's office but didn't go inside. Not without Matt. They were going to do this together like they had from the moment they found C.J. Yet, she couldn't help think about how close they'd gotten last night, and how quickly things had changed this morning.

Matt's truck pulled up at the curb and he got out. She

felt a rush of excitement, but was disappointed when he kept his distance. "Have you talked to anyone?" he asked.

She shook her head. "No, I was waiting for you."

He nodded. "Okay, let's go." He followed her inside where she saw Rick. There was a small, tired-looking woman about thirty with dark blond hair pulled back into a ponytail, sitting in a chair in the waiting area.

Rick escorted her toward them. "Alisa and Matt, this is Caden Jackson Pruett's mother, Loretta."

The slightly built woman spoke first. "Mr. Lawton told me what you've done for my son. There are no words to thank you."

Matt wasn't impressed. "Well, I would like to know why you didn't call the authorities to help get your boy back?"

The woman was taken aback. "Because, Mr. Rafferty, I was afraid. Charlie was very angry after the divorce. Every time I did call the police, they never did much, mainly because Charlie was a cop, too. So that's why I went along with what my ex-husband wanted.

"About six months ago, during one of the scheduled weekend visits, Charlie didn't bring Caden back on the Sunday night. When he'd finally contacted me hours later, he told me that he wanted to spend some time with his son, and if I called the police, he'd threatened to disappear into Mexico. I had no idea what he was capable of. If I kept quiet, he promised he'd let me talk to Caden every few days. That he would bring him home."

"Well, he didn't, did he?" Matt said. "Your husband abandoned the boy."

Something sparked in her hazel eyes. "I didn't know that until Mr. Lawton told me. If I had to do it all over again, I would have gone to the police. They never helped me much when Charlie abused me during our marriage, so I didn't have much faith that they could find my son." Tears rolled down her cheeks and she brushed them away. "All I care about is my son, Mr. Rafferty, and keeping Charlie away from him. He's the bad guy, I'm not."

She glanced at the sheriff. "Now, I need to see my son."

At noon, the sheriff, the caseworker from social services and Loretta Pruett were still sorting out the facts. Matt wasn't happy because he and Alisa didn't have any say at all. And they'd been looking after the boy.

He walked to the window and looked out onto Main Street. He saw the new neon sign that read Rafferty's Place over his restaurant. His dream. Since his return from the army, all he wanted was a simple life. With his family.

He'd needed time to heal, to lose the nightmares, forget all that he'd seen and done overseas. Over time his PTSD had gotten better. Until another nightmare last night.

He thought about Alisa. He was involved up to his eyebrows. His life had been far from simple the second he'd let Alisa get too close. He'd let her see a side of him that he hadn't shared with many. Not in a long time and that scared the hell out of him. He couldn't let her see the real him.

He turned as the door opened and saw C.J. walk into the sheriff's office escorted by Beth's daughter, Lilly and her husband, Texas Ranger, Noah Cooper. The boy ran to him. "Matt, what's wrong? Did you get arrested?"

Matt couldn't help but smile. "No, son, I didn't." He

glanced at Alisa and she came to him. "Alisa and I have something to tell you."

The boy's eyes lit up. "My dad came back?"

Alisa shook her head. "No, but there's someone here who wants to see you really badly. Your mom."

So many emotions showed across his face. "My mom?" He shook his head. "No, my mom doesn't want me. Dad said so."

C.J. tried to pull away, but Matt held on tight. "Whoa, C.J., listen to me a second. Okay?"

Finally the boy stopped fighting.

"What if your dad made a mistake? What if your mom just couldn't find you?"

Alisa knelt down beside the boy. "C.J., I know your mother has been missing you for a long time. And I think you miss her."

A tear hit the boy's cheek. "No. I don't need her."

Alisa felt her own tears welling. "Well, she needs you a lot."

"You just want to get rid of me 'cause I'm too much trouble." Another tear escaped. "Like my mom."

"No, C.J., I wanted you more than you know," she admitted. "But not as much as your real mom. She's been really sad. Sad because her boy has been gone a long time."

He sniffed and looked at Matt. "Are you going to make me go home to live with her?"

Matt shook his head. "No, but I think you should talk to her. Hear what she has to say before you make a decision."

The child looked back at Alisa. "You'll still keep me if I don't want to go?"

Alisa hesitated a moment. "C.J., you have to give her a chance."

"Okay."

The sheriff opened his door and motioned for Loretta to come in. Alisa stood and backed away as C.J. turned to her. "Mom?"

She walked toward him. "Oh, Caden," she choked out. "I missed you so much."

The tears flowed down the boy's cheeks as his mother knelt down and wrapped her child in her arms. C.J. didn't fight her, instead he held on tightly.

Alisa watched Matt and saw the tight emotions across his face. He walked out of the room. She wanted to follow, knowing how hard this was for him. He and C.J. had gotten close.

Sheriff Bradshaw took her aside. "The caseworker, Judy Thomas, has decided it would be best if she doesn't release the boy to his mother just yet. Although Mrs. Pruett has physical custody, C.J. hasn't been with her for months. I'm concerned because Charlie is still out there and he has a past record of abuse."

"Is he dangerous?"

Sheriff shrugged. "He still needs to be apprehended. We're checking with oil companies along the coast."

Her phone rang. She picked it up to hear her father's voice. She explained things to him, then talked to her mother. She extended an invitation to Loretta to come and stay at River's End.

Alisa decided that C.J.'s mother might be more comfortable at the homestead house with her son.

"I'm sure social services will be happy you're willing to keep him a little longer. And in the meantime we'll try to find Charlie."

Alisa was thinking about Matt. She hoped this would give him time to adjust to the boy leaving. They went and told the news to C.J. He looked around. "Where's Matt?"

"I'm here." He stepped back into the room. "What do you need?"

"Can we still go horseback riding?"

Matt smiled. "I promised, didn't I? I don't break my promises."

He didn't even look at her. She had a feeling that he didn't feel the same way about hearts.

It was the perfect afternoon for a ride, and Alisa hoped a perfect day for a mother and son to reconnect. Alisa took Loretta to her house first to drop off her bag while Matt took C.J. to the stables at the Triple R and to feed White Cloud.

Once Alisa's houseguest was settled in the third bedroom, where one of the twin beds from C.J.'s room had been moved in by a couple ranch hands, they left to meet the others.

As they rode to the ranch, Alisa tried not to think about the difference in Matt since the early morning phone call, but it was there in the back of her mind. It was vaguely reminiscent of what happened three years ago. It was as if he'd been handed an excuse to cool things between them.

When they arrived, Alisa put on a smile. Pete had the horses saddled, including the one she rode the last time, Carolina, and a gentle mare, Carmel, for Loretta. C.J. was on a small mare, Taffy, and the child made no bones about wanting to stick close to Matt. Alisa found she wanted to do the same but she took charge of helping Loretta. The woman wasn't an experienced rider, but caught on quickly.

Matt and C.J. led the foursome. Matt was about

twenty yards in front of her, and he'd barely given her a glance all morning. Okay, she knew that he was concerned about C.J., but wasn't she worth some time, too?

Loretta's voice broke into her thoughts, nodding toward her son. "They're pretty close, aren't they?"

"Yes, they are," she agreed. "Have been from the start. C.J. didn't want much to do with me at first, but he followed Matt around like his shadow. Not to worry, Matt's a good man and he cares about your son." Alisa glanced at Loretta. "That little guy has come to mean a lot to me, too."

Loretta gave a trembling sigh. "I'm so glad you two found him. I don't want to think about what might have happened if you hadn't."

Alisa had worried about the same thing. "We're glad we were able to locate you. C.J. needs his mother."

Loretta managed a sad smile. "I hope I can make this up to him."

"Give him some time. I think deep down your son knows you'd never really leave him, but Charlie did a good job brainwashing him."

"I've done so many things wrong," Loretta admitted. "I should have left my husband a long time ago. Every time he hit me, he always said he was sorry, blaming it on the pressures of his job. Oh, the promises he made me. And I believed him. Little did I know Charlie was telling Caden lies about me."

"That's pretty typical of an abuser," Alisa assured her.

"It's no excuse to stay. I didn't have anywhere to go if I did leave. I was a waitress and the restaurant where I worked helped me get away and get legal advice for the divorce. I asked for help to find Caden, but I was so afraid Charlie might do something crazy."

Loretta eyed her closely. "Am I too late to get my son back?" she asked as her horse shifted and Alisa instructed her how to get the mare back on the trail.

"I don't think so. I believe C.J. knows how you feel about him." She thought about Matt and how his mother hadn't wanted him or any of her family.

Alisa glanced up ahead to see Matt and Caden laughing and she got a funny feeling in her chest. The man would make a great father. She glanced away, knowing she had to stop dreaming about a future with Matt.

That evening, Alisa drove Loretta and C.J. back to the house. She sent the child off to take a bath, and was grateful he didn't put up his usual fight. Ten minutes later, he was in pajamas and in bed. She gave him a hug, something the boy had only recently permitted. She'd looked forward to them, too. Now it looked like those would be ending when he returned home with his mother. She'd be losing two men in her life. Not that either were ever hers.

Loretta walked into the bedroom, and Alisa left mother and son to their bedtime ritual. She went off to her own room and busied herself with work when there was a knock on the front door.

She tried not to get excited thinking it might be Matt. He was probably only here to see C.J.

"Hi," he said when she opened the door.

Her breath caught in her throat for a second and she managed a nod.

"You got a minute?" he asked.

She stepped aside and allowed him into the living room.

He turned and asked, "Is everyone in bed?"

"Yes, and I'm about to head that way myself." She avoided looking in his eyes.

"I waited to come by a little later so we wouldn't be disturbed. I need to talk to you."

She didn't want to hear his speech again. "Loretta is here."

"Good, then she can stay with C.J.." He took her hand and pulled her outside into the cool, spring evening and closed the door behind them. "We need to clear up some things."

She pulled her hand away. "There's nothing to clear up. I didn't ask for anything from you, nor did I expect it. Did you think I would?"

Matt knew he deserved that. "I'm not sure I can be what you want me to be. I'm not ready—"

"For what, Matt?" she interrupted. "I don't remember asking for anything. You're the one who showed up at my apartment last night."

He sighed and combed his fingers through his hair. "I can see I've already messed things up."

She folded her arms. "You mean by acting as if I didn't exist today?"

"That wasn't my intention. It's just C.J.'s mother coming kind of took center stage, don't you think?"

"Good excuse," she told him. "Soon you won't have to have one, because by the looks of things C.J. will return home with his mother. And we won't be spending time together."

He sighed. "I never said I didn't want to spend time with you. A relationship wouldn't be a good idea right now."

"Maybe you're not willing to work at it, or stick around long enough to see if things *could* work out."

Matt caught his breath as he looked at her bathed in

the fading light. All he wanted to do was pull her into his arms. He couldn't do that. Not yet. "Alisa, there are things I need to handle by myself right now."

"I could help you."

He couldn't do that to her. "It's better this way, Alisa."

"Better? For me, or for you?" she pressed.

"For you, Alisa."

"Don't say that, Matt. Don't try to tell me what's good for me. You have no idea." She swallowed, then said, "Goodbye, Matt."

He could only watch her go back into the house and close the door, closing him away from ever having her in his life.

He told himself he was better off to leave now. So he did what he'd always done in the past. He turned and walked away from everything he'd ever dreamed of having.

Alisa managed to make it into her bedroom before tears fell. She was angrier with herself than him. Matt had tried to tell her how he was. Twice. But she'd refused to listen.

Instead she went and fell in love with him once again. Maybe she never stopped. Now she had no choice. She couldn't let Matt Rafferty keep breaking her heart.

A soft knock on the door caused her to wipe her eyes. "Come in."

Loretta peered in through the door. "I'm sorry to bother you, Alisa, but I couldn't help but hear you crying." She frowned. "I hope I haven't caused you any stress."

Alisa crossed the room. "Oh, no, Loretta. There's

been a lot going on these past few weeks. It finally came to a head. I'm okay." She put on a smile. "Really."

Loretta nodded, but didn't move. "You know, as an innocent observer, the two of you seem to care about each other."

How did she know anything about them? "It's more one-sided."

"It was C.J. who said whenever you two were together you acted weird." The woman smiled. "And I watched all day how Matt tried to ignore you, but his gaze followed you around everywhere you went." She looked sad. "I'm sorry if my coming here has caused problems between the two of you."

"No, Loretta, it's not you. Matt and I have history, and finding C.J. threw us back together again…temporarily."

"Too bad. He seems like a good man. C.J. was lucky to have a good male role model these past weeks." She smiled. "And now, I've got my son back. It's not going to be easy. But hopefully with counseling we'll get through what his father did, along with his abandonment issues." Loretta sighed. "It's hard to know where to begin."

Alisa went to her. "It's going to be all right, Loretta. You can stay here as long as you need."

The woman couldn't hide her sadness. "I can't move into your home, you barely know me. Besides, I need to go back to Amarillo, to my job."

"Why? You said you don't have any family back there. C.J. has made a lot of friends here. He's doing well in school and he's almost caught up with his grade."

"He's a smart boy," Loretta said.

Suddenly Alisa got an idea. "Loretta, if you could find a job here in town and a place to live, would you consider staying?"

The blonde shook her head. "I can't afford to come up with the deposit for an apartment. As for a job, I wouldn't know where to begin."

Alisa raised an eyebrow. "How about my apartment in town? You and C.J. could use it for a few months. And I might have a few job connections. You wouldn't happen to know how to quilt, would you?"

Loretta studied her. "My grandmother taught me years ago, but I'm only an amateur."

"Come on, how about a cup of tea? And I'll tell you all about the neighborhood quilt shop, the Blind Stitch."

"Sure." Loretta followed her into the small kitchen. Alisa filled the kettle and set it on the stove.

"A good friend of mine is Jenny Rafferty," Alisa began. "She's Matt's sister-in-law, and she's the manager. She's always looking for part-time help."

"Alisa, I'm grateful you want to help us, but I'm going to need more than part-time work."

Alisa thought about a waitress jobs in town. Of course the first restaurant that came to mind was Rafferty's Place. He might be able to help. "You know Matt owns a restaurant. He might have a job for you."

Loretta's hazel eyes lit up. "Now that, I have years of experience doing."

Alisa took two mugs from the cupboard and placed the tea bags inside. She was about to pour the hot water when there was a sound on the porch. She paused. Someone was out there. Had Matt come back?

Excitement surged through her. "I wonder who that could be?" she said as she went to the door. Not even thinking of any danger, she opened the door to find a stranger. But was he?

Fear struck as she came face-to-face with a man who could only be Charlie Jackson. She tried to slam

the door, but he hit it with his hand and swung it open.
"Well, well, you must be Alisa Merrick."

"What do you want?"

"Only what's mine, my family."

CHAPTER TWELVE

IT WAS nearly midnight as Matt wandered around his house unable to sleep. He couldn't get Alisa out of his head, or stop seeing her face before he walked away.

He went into the kitchen, opened the refrigerator and reached for a beer. He twisted off the top and took a long drink. This was the last thing he needed to do. He had to get up early to help move the herd.

There was a knock on the back door and his brother peered in. "Hey, I saw your light. Is there a problem?"

"No, just too much going on today." Hell, his entire life was a mess. "I'm still keyed up. It's been a long day and another one tomorrow."

Evan pulled out a bar stool and sat down. "You'll miss C.J. We'll all miss the kid, but you have to be happy he's back with his mother."

"Yeah, if you say so."

Evan was quiet for a while, then said, "Of course that won't give you an excuse to hang around with Alisa. You'll have to come up with something new."

Matt jerked his head up. "Funny."

"Why don't you just admit you have feelings for the woman?" He raised a hand. "Don't bother to deny it."

He didn't. "We'll never work."

"This *is* serious." Evan went to the refrigerator,

grabbed a beer, then came back to the counter. "Now, start at the beginning, I want to hear how my brother bites the dust and falls for one woman."

Matt didn't want to think about his feelings for Alisa. "We're not good for each other. We never were."

"Whoa." Evan waved the longneck bottle. "How long has this been going on?" Matt filled him in on how he'd gotten together with Alisa three years ago.

His brother whistled. "I have to say, you've got great taste in women. Does Alisa feel the same?"

"Not so sure, now." He took a drink, the beer tasted bitter. "It's probably for the best."

"Why? You can't think a Rafferty isn't good enough for a Merrick."

"Of course not." Maybe, he thought. "I'm not the kind of guy who would be good at following Alisa to Austin, much less Washington."

"I thought Alisa was only running for town council."

"She's a Merrick. They go to Washington."

"Have you talked to her about this?"

He shrugged, but didn't say anything.

Evan leaned forward. "What's the real reason you're here and not with her? Is it your nightmares?"

"Doesn't matter to her." He couldn't forget the feel of her arms around him. He shook it away and looked at his brother. "I haven't done well when it comes to long-term."

"Man, you haven't stuck around long enough with a woman to find out. Not since…" Evan looked thoughtful. "Jody? Don't tell me this is about that spoiled, little cheerleader?"

Matt thought back to the girl who drove him crazy. "It's not just her." He paused, then stood up and walked to the window over the stink. "There's Mom." God, he hated feeling like his guts were being ripped out.

Evan came to him. "You always had a big ego, little brother. What makes you think you're so special that Patty Rafferty's leaving was because of you?"

Matt stared at his brother.

Evan grew serious. "She left me, too. You don't think I don't wonder if I caused her to go away? What about Dad? He's had to carry the guilt that he caused his wife, not only to leave him, but his boys, too."

"I guess I never thought about that." He remembered his dad's sadness, but they never talked much about it. He looked back at Evan. "What about you? How did you get over it? How were you able to move on and love Jenny?"

He smiled sadly. "Wasn't easy. I messed up a lot of times. But in the end, I wanted her love. She helped me heal a lot of wounds."

Matt envied Evan for the family he had.

"Look," Evan stressed. "I'm not saying it was easy. Love's a risk, but it's the only way you get the woman."

Matt felt a surge of hope, but it was dashed again. "I've really messed up. I'm not sure I can fix things with Alisa."

He nodded. "Jenny gave me more chances than I deserved. Women want to know that you love them enough that you'll be there."

For the first time in a long time, Matt felt hope. "You'd better know how lucky you are," Matt told him.

"I do. I count my blessings every day." Evan grinned. "In fact I came out here to share more good news with you. Jenny and I are having another baby."

"Hey, that's great!" Matt was excited. He grabbed

his brother and gave him a bear hug. What would it be like to share this kind of miracle with Alisa?

"Thanks. It wasn't exactly planned this soon," Evan said. "But, yeah, my life is pretty much perfect and I wish the same for you. But you've got to take the chance, Matt. Talk to Alisa."

Matt nodded, feeling free for the first time in a long time. "I will." He wanted to rush back to Alisa's house and beg her to listen to what he had to say.

His cell phone rang. "Who the hell?" He looked at the caller ID. Alisa.

"Alisa?"

"Matt." It wasn't Alisa but C.J.

"C.J. what's wrong?"

"My dad's here. I'm scared, Matt." He heard the fear in his voice. "I think he's going to hurt my mom and Alisa."

His pulse raced at the thought of Charlie Jackson anywhere near Alisa. "It's okay, buddy. Where are you?"

"I'm in Alisa's bedroom."

"Climb out the window, son. Hide by the big oak. I'll be there in no time." He hung up and looked at Evan. "Charlie's at Alisa's place."

"Let's go." His brother pulled out his phone, and called the sheriff as they rushed out the door. Matt prayed that he had enough time to get to Alisa and pull her out of harm's way. He also promised that he would let her know how he truly felt about her.

He prayed he wouldn't be too late.

"You'd be better off if you just leave now," Alisa told Charlie. "Take my car before anyone knows you're here."

Charlie kept pacing back and forth, occasionally stopping to make more demands of them. He looked tired, much older than his age. His blond hair was dirty. Thank God C.J. was in the bedroom.

"This is all your fault." He waved the gun at Loretta, then at Alisa. "If you hadn't nosed around in my business… I had someone taking care of my boy."

"Your son was living on the streets."

"I was coming back. How was I supposed to know that my neighbor would get arrested? But you sent that investigator down to the Gulf, asking questions about me."

"Charlie, please leave Alisa out of this," Loretta said. "Take me. I'll go with you."

He glared at his ex-wife. "Why would you think I would want you anymore?" He walked over and without warning, slapped her across the face. Loretta cried out as she sank back against the sofa.

Alisa stared at the piece of scum, waiting for her own blow. She wasn't going to give him the satisfaction of cowering. But Charlie only called her a derogatory name and walked toward the window.

Alisa looked at Loretta and saw her mouth was bleeding. They needed to get help. The River's End Ranch was gated, but Charlie had bragged about how he managed to hide in the back of a ranch hand's truck coming from town to get onto the property.

Now she needed to get him out of here, but she knew he would be taking hostages, at the very least his son, probably his ex-wife. She eyed the gun and thought that she could possibly die. And C.J. if she let him go with his father.

No! She wouldn't die, none of them would, not if she

could help it. "Charlie, you know my daddy is a retired U.S. Senator."

"Big deal. It's not going to help you."

"It could help you. He has a helicopter and the pilot on call. He could fly you to Mexico. Even add some money to help you get a new start."

The man looked interested.

"Let me call my dad." She was working to keep the trembling out of her voice. "Give me an hour to put this together."

"Get on the phone," he ordered.

"First you have to make me a promise."

He looked angry, but she rushed on. "Leave C.J. here. He's a kid. Besides, he'll only slow you down."

Charlie looked confused as if he were on drugs. "Fine," he growled. "But your daddy better come through. Get your phone."

"It's in my bedroom." She pointed down the hall. "My purse is just inside the door."

"Be fast. I won't hesitate to come after you and you won't like what will happen."

Alisa walked down the hall to her room. The bedside lamp was on and her purse was on the bed. She went to reach for it, but someone caught her from behind and covered her mouth.

"It's me, Matt," he whispered in her ear. "C.J. is safely out of here."

He released her and she turned to see him. She fought her tears, grateful he was here.

"You're safe now, Alisa. Come on, I'll help you out the window."

"No!" she gasped. "I can't leave Loretta. Charlie will kill her."

"He could kill you, too. I can't let you go back in there."

She wanted so badly to go with Matt. "I'm sorry, I've got to get back."

"Okay." He handed her the phone. "Call your dad just as planned. He's aware of the situation." Matt squeezed her hand. "I don't like it, Alisa, so listen to me. When Charlie takes you and Loretta outside, we need a clear shot to take him out."

"Matt, I think he's on drugs."

He breathed a curse. "Okay, this is important. When I call your name, you drop to the ground. Try to get the message to Loretta, too."

She nodded and took one last look at him. "Got it." She walked out of the bedroom, wondering if she'd ever see this man again.

She handed the phone to Charlie. He went through the saved numbers, and punched the redial and handed it to her. "Make it short and to the point. Your hour starts now."

Alisa put the phone to her ear, hoping to distract Charlie as she walked toward the front door. "Hi, Dad. It's Alisa."

"Hi, sweetheart. What's up?"

"I need some help." She went on to tell him about the deal she'd made with the man holding a gun on her.

"You got it. Now let me talk to Charlie."

Alisa handed the phone to him. "The senator wants to talk to you."

He grabbed the phone. "Yeah."

"Mr. Pruett, you'll get everything that my daughter promised, but if you hurt Alisa, I will track you down. You aren't going to like the end result. Is that understood?"

"Just get me the damn helicopter," Charlie demanded and cut the connection. He tossed the phone on the sofa and glanced at the clock. "You got fifty minutes left."

Alisa wanted to run back into the bedroom and into the safety of Matt's arms.

Matt drew on all the skill he'd learned over his years in the military, but this situation was different. There were two defenseless women out there. One he'd never gotten the chance to tell how he truly felt about her. The other was a young mother who needed to be around to raise her son. Then throw in one crazed guy with a gun and they had a disaster just waiting to happen.

He had to stop Charlie Jackson, and there wasn't any room for error. If he made any mistakes, he could lose them all.

He spotted Bradshaw at the window and the sheriff motioned for him to come outside.

Matt didn't want to leave, but knew if he was discovered there could be more trouble. He listened at the bedroom door a minute. He didn't like this one bit. This could go bad in an instant. He wasn't going to let that happen, if he could help it. He crossed the room, climbed out the window and dropped to the ground. He met the sheriff and his brother at the back of the house.

"You couldn't get her out?"

Matt shook his head. "No, she's too stubborn. Afraid Jackson would hurt Loretta."

Bradshaw jammed his fist on his hips. "Damn, we don't need everyone around here, trying to play hero. That helicopter is due in ten minutes," he told him. "It's more than likely Charlie will try to take a hostage with him. So do the ladies at least know what to do?"

Matt nodded. "You can't let that bird leave the

ground with either one of them in it. So that only gives
us maybe thirty seconds to get a shot off on our target
moving across an open pasture."

"Whoa. Whoa. You and Evan shouldn't even be
here," Bradshaw said.

"I'm sure as hell not leaving. Alisa thinks he's on
drugs. Besides, I'm the next best thing you've got to a
sharpshooter."

The sheriff shook his head. "And a civilian. We
called in Noah Cooper. It's been cleared with his company in San Antonio, so as of now the Texas Rangers
are in charge of this operation. Coop's already in posi-
tion to take the shot. So you Raffertys need to stay out
of the way."

"Like hell. I told Alisa I would give her a signal to
drop to the ground. I'm following this through."

Bradshaw sighed. "Then go to Coop and listen for
his instructions. There are lives in danger."

Matt knew that better than anyone. Alisa was everything to him. Was he too late to finally tell her?

Alisa watched Charlie Jackson pace the room. He was
getting impatient and that worried her more. She also
wondered if Matt was still in her bedroom. Was he
going to risk his life to try to save them? She didn't want
that, either. The only other alternative was that she and
Loretta had to get out of this. Thank God, she'd been
able to relay Matt's instructions to her.

Someone was going to shoot Charlie. Although she
didn't like it, it looked to be their only chance to survive.
She fought tears thinking about her family and the new
niece or nephew she might not meet. And Matt. Alisa's
thoughts were suddenly interrupted by the sound of the
approaching helicopter.

The phone rang and Charlie answered it. "Yeah, I hear. When it lands there better not be a soul around or your daughter is history." He snapped the phone shut. "Let's go."

Alisa looked at Loretta then stood. Charlie grabbed his ex-wife first. "Don't try anything, because I'd like nothing more than to get rid of you." He grabbed Alisa next and she moved without any pushing. "You're my insurance policy, little miss daughter of Senator Merrick," he said. "I think we're going to get to know each other real well."

Alisa had to fight to stay calm. The last thing she wanted was to show Charlie fear. He would enjoy it too much. Worse, he had the advantage and she was going to fight like hell to get out of this. Alive.

After peering through the window, Charlie opened the door, and pulled Loretta out first as a shield, then he put himself between them. A rank body odor nearly gagged her. She swallowed hard, and kept telling herself that Matt was out there.

Charlie nudged them. "Okay, all together, and walk slowly."

They did as he told them. Alisa listened for the sound of Matt's voice, but the noise of the helicopter's blades and her pulse pounding in her ears made it difficult to hear anything else.

With Charlie wedged between them so tight she couldn't even talk to Loretta, they made their way across the ankle-high grass. The only light came from the helicopter about thirty feet away.

Alisa knew time was running out, then suddenly she heard Matt's command, "Alisa!"

Alisa dropped to the ground, shoving Loretta out of the way. The last thing she remembered was another command to Charlie to drop his weapon, then there was the sound of shots.

Then everything went black.

"Alisa! Alisa! Wake up, darlin'."

Alisa groaned and blinked her eyes open. "Matt." She gasped and tried to sit up. "What happened?" She looked around and discovered she was in her house on the sofa. Matt was sitting in front of her.

"It's over," he told her. "Charlie's can't hurt you again."

"He's dead?"

He nodded slowly. "There wasn't any other choice and no time. Charlie had his gun pointed at Loretta."

"Oh, God," she gasped and sat up. "Loretta?"

"She's fine, too. One of the deputies took her to see C.J. at your parents' house."

Alisa released a breath, but it didn't stop her shaking. "I don't think I've ever been so scared."

Matt nodded. "We don't know what makes someone go off like this, but by the looks of it, Charlie wanted it to end this way."

Suddenly she felt the burning in her eyes, but she refused to cry. She wouldn't fall apart now. A bit wobbly, she fought to stand up. She refused Matt's help because she had to do this on her own. Even though unsteady, she walked to the fireplace, seeing the bright stoplights outside from a patrol car out the window. "I can't believe any of this happened."

Matt was right behind her. "I thought the same thing. When you walked back into that room with Jackson, I nearly went crazy. It took everything in me to keep from going after you."

She closed her eyes, feeling good hearing his words.

Matt followed her. "You're safe now."

He reached out for her. She wanted nothing more than to sink into his protective warmth, but she couldn't. It would be too easy to lean on him, to let him take her home and back into his bed. How long would it last? Another weekend? She pulled away. "And I appreciate your help tonight. But I'm fine now."

He didn't back off. "Alisa, I want to be here for you. When I saw that man's hands on you…" He paused. "Please let me help."

"Matt, it's better if I go to my family."

"I care about you," he said, his voice whispered tones.

She turned around and was hit with his mesmerizing blue eyes. She saw concern, but was there love?

She had to fight to keep from falling in his arms. "But for how long this time?" She paused for a beat. "Another night in your bed, then you're gone again?"

He started to speak and she stopped him. "No, I'm not trying to guilt you into anything. I'm just stating a fact. I can't be your woman when it's convenient for you. I deserve better."

He only stared at her, and then there was a sound of commotion before the front door opened. Her mother and father rushed in as Matt stepped back.

Her mother got to her first. "Oh, God, Alisa," she began. "We've been so afraid."

Alisa let her tears fall. "I'm not going to lie, I was terrified. How is Loretta?"

Her dad answered, "She's fine, and so is C.J." He shook his head. "We weren't sure if they'd be able to pull this off. The sheriff said you pushed Loretta to the ground so Coop could get the shot off."

Alisa nodded. "Matt told me to do it."

Her father frowned. "When did you talk to him?"

She motioned toward the hall. "He was hiding in my bedroom when I went in to get my cell phone. I think C.J. called him when his dad showed up here."

The senator nodded. "That little guy did a good job. I also owe a big thanks to Matt." Her father looked around. "Where is he?"

Alisa scanned the room but didn't see him. Why didn't that surprise her? She should be used to his disappearing act. But it still hurt.

The past few nights had been rough on Matt, but probably not as bad as for Alisa. Every time he closed his eyes he kept seeing her falling to the ground and Jackson holding a weapon. He prayed that Alisa was doing okay. That she'd been able to talk with someone who could help her get through it.

His own solution had been physical labor at the ranch. It might have helped clear his head, but he couldn't get Alisa out of his heart. He'd screwed up. He was grateful he had plenty to do to keep his mind occupied.

It was about noon when he finished at the ranch and headed into town. So far they'd only be open in the afternoons for bar service and evenings for meals. Maybe later, he'd serve lunch.

He walked though the back door to find Loretta Pruett seated at the counter, talking with Kevin.

His bartender saw him first. "Matt, good you're here early."

"Got finished with the chores." He turned to the other person. "Hello, Loretta. How are you doing?"

"Hi, Matt. I'm fine. I don't want to disturb you, but if you have the time could we talk?"

"Of course." He looked back at Kevin. "I'll be in the bar if you need me."

He escorted Loretta through the double doors. "I didn't expect to see you today. Where's C.J.?"

"He went back to school. So I thought it would be a good time to stop by."

"Sure." He walked her into the bar section of the restaurant. "You want a soft drink or something?"

"Maybe some water."

He went behind the bar and poured her a glass. After she took a drink, she looked at him. "I know you don't like me much." When he started to disagree, she stopped him. "It's okay, because I haven't liked myself much, either." She took another drink. "I want you to know that since C.J. and I have been given a second chance I plan to start a new life here."

Matt frowned. "You're not returning to Amarillo?"

"Only for Charlie's funeral since he has no family. It's for C.J. mostly. He needs the closure."

Poor kid. "How's he handling all this?"

She shrugged. "He acts tough, but of course, he's hurting."

"You want me to talk to him?"

She looked hopeful. "You wouldn't mind?"

Matt shook his head, remembering how he'd felt after his mother left. He didn't want C.J. to carry that guilt. "You know I care about the boy."

"Thank you." She hesitated, then said, "Alisa has been talking to me about all the benefits of small town living."

Matt smiled, knowing Alisa would probably take her under her wing. "That's good. C.J. is doing well here."

"Now, all I need is a job," Loretta began. "Alisa said the Blind Stitch hires, but it's only part-time."

"I might be looking for a lunch waitress," he blurted out. "I mean, it will be a few weeks yet before I'm ready to open during the day, but I'll need someone."

"You'd consider hiring me?"

"I hear you've got experience. When you get back from Amarillo come see me."

Oh, boy, now he had a day-shift waitress and nothing else. Maybe his dad would help him out afternoons. And he'd have Pete hire more help at the ranch.

He thought about Alisa. He wished the problems with her were that easy to solve.

CHAPTER THIRTEEN

A FEW days later, Alisa and walked through the doors of the Blind Stitch with Loretta. As much as she loved the feel of this place, she'd never got the quilting bug.

"Well, what do you think?" She glanced at her new friend.

"Oh, my. This is wonderful."

Loretta—who had asked to be called Lori—looked ten years younger since her return from town. The pretty blonde was only a year older than she was, but the emotional abuse by her ex-husband had her not caring about her appearance. It seemed that was changing.

"The owner, Allison, had a great vision when she came to town a few years back. Now she's married to my boss, Alex Casali, and with young twins she doesn't work anymore. You'll meet the manager, Jenny, today."

Lori seemed nervous. "Could I look around a minute?"

"Knock yourself out."

Alisa left her and went into the connecting room where the ladies of the Quilters Corner sat at their usual table at the storefront windows. That was where she found her mother and Beth.

She put on a smile when she saw her mother. Louisa

stood and hugged her. "How are you doing, *querida?* You haven't been by the house in a few days."

"I've been busy at work." Dear Lord, she'd just lied to her mother. "I'll come this weekend."

Louisa looked into her daughter's eyes. "You're not sleeping. I knew you went back to your house too soon."

"Mom, once the sheriff finished with the investigation, I had to go back. I can't let that man drive me out of my home." Another lie. It wasn't Charlie Jackson, but Matt who kept her awake nights. "It's getting better."

Louisa stroked her cheek. "It's just that you'll always be my baby. And I worry."

She hugged her mother, knowing how blessed she'd been having her family. "I love you for it."

"And I love you. So does your father. He wants to help with the election since you only have a week to go."

"Honestly, Mom, I haven't even given it a thought."

Her mother gave her a strange look. "Okay." She brushed her hair back. "You know if there's anything you need to talk about, I'm here."

Alisa managed a nod. She couldn't get any words past the lump in her throat.

There was some commotion and Alisa turned to see Sean Rafferty, his hands full with a carryout box. He grinned as he walked to Beth and kissed her right on the mouth.

"I guess I need to bring lunch more often." He winked at Beth and turned to them. "Hi, Louisa." He set the box of food on the table and pulled Alisa into a big hug. "This is a wonderful surprise, lass. And since you're here, you can help us sample Matt's new lunch menu."

No! She couldn't see him today. "Thank you for the offer, Sean, but I can't stay."

"Sean, she's busy with the campaign. Not that she has anything to worry about."

"I haven't won yet." She wasn't sure if she had the desire to keep going.

"Bite your tongue, daughter," Louisa said. "Of course you'll win. You're a Merrick."

Out of the corner of her eye, she caught someone and turned to find Matt. Her breath hitched as she watched him talking with Lori. He suddenly laughed and Alisa's chest tightened. Matt turned in her direction and his smile faded. He started cross the room toward her.

She panicked and grabbed her purse. "Mom, I really need to go." She hurried past the group including Matt. When he called to her, she kept on walking.

Matt watched Alisa say something to Lori then she headed out the door. Without a backward glance she was gone.

Matt went outside and looked up and down the street. He spotted Alisa behind the wheel of her car. He waved and called to her, but she only sped away from the curb. He cursed as she raced down Main Street. It hurt. She couldn't stand to be around him.

The door to the shop opened and his father walked out. He looked concerned. "Son, you okay?"

He shook his head. "No. I've messed up big time. Sometimes you think you're doing the right thing, and realized you blew your chance."

Sean looked down Main Street. "I've been there, son. The thing is to find a way to change it."

"I've tried. She won't talk to me."

"A Rafferty giving up?" He nodded to the empty street. "You've had it pretty easy when it comes to women. Now, a woman that's important to you is a different story. So it's up to you to change the ending. Go after her, son. Tell her how you feel," he stressed. "Tell her your true feelings—promise you'll love her for a lifetime." He paused. "It is for a lifetime, isn't it?"

Matt hesitated, then realized he never wanted to be without her. "Yes. I want it all with Alisa."

His father smiled again. "Now you just have to convince her that you're the perfect guy for her."

"Got any ideas?"

"Oh, lad, you were blessed with the Rafferty charm, so use it."

CHAPTER FOURTEEN

IT WAS finally Sunday afternoon and Alisa walked through the barn at River's End, leading her favorite mare, Bonnie Sue. She was looking forward to a long hard ride after a long week of work, and a Saturday morning spent with her father campaigning door-to-door. All the time listening to him talk about when she ran for state office, when she ran for the U.S. Senate. She could barely make it through the local election.

Yes, she needed this ride. She needed to thank Sloan for suggesting they go together. She walked into the corral and instead of her brother found her dad talking with the ranch foreman, Bud.

He came toward her. "You're going riding now?"

She nodded. "With Sloan. I need to clear my head."

He watched her like everyone had since the Charlie Jackson incident. "Are you okay? You look tired."

"Dad, really, I'm fine." She tied her horse at the railing wondering where her brother was. "And, yes, I am tired, this is my first day off in a week."

"Well, it's a busy time." He smiled. "You can rest after the election next week."

She nodded. "I'm thinking I might even visit friends just to get out of town." She needed time away from Matt, too.

"Now, you can't take too much time off," he warned. "We need to start the PR on the Boys and Girls Club. It doesn't hurt to let the legislators in Austin know what you're up to."

"Dad, my priority right now will be to get the okay from the council to start remodeling the Club. Alex can get a crew together to start the work immediately. That's my main focus. The kids."

Clay Merrick eyed her closely. "This kind of press can't be bought, especially if you want to move on to bigger and better things. You do want that, don't you, Alisa?"

"Do I have to decide now? Can't I just enjoy serving on the council?"

He frowned and asked, "How long has this been going on? And why the change of heart?"

Since she'd realized how much she cared about this town and wanted to build a life here. "It's not a change of heart exactly. It's more like a pause."

Suddenly her brother appeared and she nearly jumped into his arms. "Sloan. There you are." She looked behind him. Where was his horse?

"Hey, son," the senator greeted him. "I need your help here. Tell Alisa that if she wants a career in public office, she can't relax now that she has some momentum."

"Can't do that, Dad. Alisa has to make her own decisions." Her brother looked at her. "What is it, sis?"

She felt her heart sink into her stomach, but she managed to look at her dad. "I'm sorry, Dad. I tried, but all I really want is to stay here in Kerry Springs."

The senator eyed her closely. "A lot has happened recently. Like you said, you're tired. You could change your mind."

Alisa couldn't back down now. "Maybe, but it's doubtful. Okay, I enjoyed following you around on the campaign trail when I was a kid, but now that I've come face-to-face with the prospect of dedicating my life to public service, I realize, it isn't for me." Her eyes filled with tears. "I'm sorry, Dad. I know you're disappointed."

"Oh, Alisa, I've never been, nor ever will be disappointed in you." He pulled her into a big hug. "I'm so proud of all you've accomplished," he whispered. "I can't lie and say I wouldn't love to see you follow in my footsteps, but this is your choice. Your life."

"Oh, Daddy. I love you."

"I love you, too, Alisa."

"Well, you sure let her off the hook easy," Sloan teased. "You rode me for months, for years, about following the long line of Merricks into politics."

Alisa stood back, knowing her bother was trying to lighten the mood. "That's because I'm Daddy's favorite."

Sloan tried to work up a glare. "Just wait until the grandbaby comes, then we'll both be out of the will."

Clay Merrick laughed as he wrapped his arms around the shoulders of his children. "I love this family." When Alisa's horse danced restlessly, he looked down at his daughter. "Hey, Bonnie Sue is getting restless, you should go on that ride. I need to get back to your mother. We have plans for dinner tonight." They waved as Clay Merrick walked back to the barn.

Alisa turned to her brother. "Where's your horse?"

"I'm not going with you, sis," he said as he escorted her toward her horse. "In fact, I never planned to go."

She stood there and waited for an explanation.

He pulled a piece of paper from his pocket. "Matt

was the one who suggested the ride. I was supposed to take you to meet up with him, but I can't do it."

Her heart began to race.

"He wants to talk to you, Alisa."

She shook her head. "I can't."

Sloan rushed on to say, "I know he hurt you, and I want to rope him and drag him behind a horse for that. But I believe he's truly sorry."

"Why are you suddenly in Matt's corner?"

"Because how many times did I mess up with Jade? Sometimes a guy needs a second chance." He handed her the note and walked away.

Alisa's hand was shaking as she opened it. "It can't end like this. Please, meet me at Sunset Ridge."

For the last hour, Matt had ridden back and forth along the ridge. He'd almost given up hope that Sloan would convince Alisa to come talk with him. Why should she? He was a bad bet any way he looked at it.

Suddenly he saw her coming over the rise. She was sitting on top of her horse, her ebony hair blowing in the breeze. Her gray Stetson was pushed low on her head as she rode toward him.

As she slowed Bonnie Sue to a walk, he grew more nervous. He didn't want to lose her now, but what if he couldn't make her stay. What if she didn't want him any longer?

She stopped about ten feet away.

"Hi. Glad you could make it."

"I'm here, but I'm not sure it isn't a waste of time."

"Give me ten minutes."

He waited several heartbeats, then she climbed off her horse. "So what do you want to say to me?"

"A lot of things." He dismounted, too. He took a few

breaths as he looked out at the beautiful grazing land, grateful when he felt Alisa come up beside him.

Matt could only stare at her beauty as he felt adrenaline rushing through him. He hated that he was so nervous.

He glanced away, trying to find the right words. Then when Alisa turned to head back toward her horse, he knew he had to say something fast. To make her realize how much he cared about her.

Alisa kept walking, not knowing what else to do. She couldn't just stand here and make small talk. Matt needed to give her a little encouragement. Please, call me back, she prayed as she walked toward Bonnie Sue.

"Don't go, Alisa."

She stopped but didn't turn around.

Then he came up behind her. "You're the first woman in a long time I've wanted to risk it all for. I want to be with you, Alisa."

Alisa could hear the pain in his voice and she faced him. His blue eyes were filled with anguish and he swallowed hard.

He continued. "I broke all my rules with you."

He glanced away, then back at her. "Years ago, I swore I'd never let anyone get close, that no one would be important to me again. Not after my mother left us." He paused. "I let another woman into my life."

"Jody," she said.

He nodded. "We had a lot of plans. I thought we did. When I failed her, she walked away without a glance. After that, I decided that I'd always be the one to leave. And I joined the army."

She swallowed the ache in her throat, feeling his pain.

He went on to say, "Three years ago when I ran into

you that night at the Roadhouse I knew I should have left you alone." He looked back at her. "But I couldn't. You drew me like no other woman I'd ever met. You don't know how close I came to breaking my rule that weekend. You made me want to make promises that I knew I couldn't keep. I had a war to fight. Hell, I wasn't sure I'd even be coming back."

Alisa went to him. "I would have written you, waited for you, Matt."

"Dear Lord, woman. That surely would have gotten me into trouble. I couldn't be thinking of you and do my job. I had to stay sane. Then when I returned from overseas, I called and when you didn't return my calls…" He shut his eyes a moment. "You wouldn't listen to me, to any explanation."

She held his gaze, hoping he could feel her love and compassion for the boy and now the man. "I thought I was owed for you to come in person and apologize."

He glanced away. "The war changed things and me. I had my own demons to fight."

She reached up and touched his face. "That wouldn't have mattered, Matt. I wouldn't ever judge you."

He released another breath. "I know you would have, but I wasn't ready to share that part of me.

"Post-Traumatic Stress Disorder," she said. "A lot of soldiers have it after they return. When we talked that night in bed, I thought it helped you."

He nodded slowly. "It did. I don't like to share that part of me." He shrugged. "My nightmares are from a time that I want to forget, not drag you into."

"At least I know why you weren't in bed with me. It had nothing to do with not wanting me?"

"Oh, God, no. Making love to you was incredible."

Alisa was so close Matt had trouble not reaching for her. "I didn't want to leave you."

"Then why did you leave?"

"Trust."

She was hurt. "You didn't trust me?"

"No, I didn't trust myself. To cover my insecurities, I felt there was safety in numbers."

"Yes, your reputation with women is legendary."

"Not as legendary as you think. I dated a lot, but haven't been with that many women. And since you, the number might surprise you."

She sobered. "Matt, I can't be that woman in your bed when it suits you."

Did she really think that's all she was to him? "It's never been that way with you, Alisa."

That gave him enough encouragement to reach for her, and tugged her against him. "I've noticed you for years, but you're a Merrick. Your father was a U.S. senator. Oh, darlin', there was no way I was getting close to you."

"So, I shouldn't tell you that I was so crazy in love with you since high school?"

Oh, God. His arms tightened around her. He looked into her velvet-brown eyes and could barely hold it together. "What about now? I've got a few more miles on me, and a lot of flaws. Could you love this guy now?"

He couldn't manage to draw a breath, then she nodded.

"Yeah? You sure about that?" He didn't wait for her answer. He removed her hat and leaned down, then brushed his lips over hers. Feeling her shiver, he pulled back to see the desire mirrored in her eyes. He captured her mouth again and drew her tight against him. Her arms went around his neck and he deepened the kiss.

When his tongue slipped inside to taste her sweetness, she whimpered and her arms moved around his back, pressing her closer. The kiss got even more heated.

Finally he broke away and they were both breathless. "You're the only woman who's ever mattered to me, Alisa. I love you and I don't want to live without you."

Alisa pulled back, afraid to believe this was happening. "Say it again, Matt Rafferty. I want to make sure I heard you right."

He cupped her face in his hands. "I love you, Alisa Merrick, and I don't want to live without you."

"I love you, too, Matt." She blinked back tears. "Wait. What exactly does all this mean?"

"I want you in my life." He grew serious. "I know how much you want a political life and I never want to stand in your way."

Alisa was touched by this man. "That will never happen. Besides, you are a decorated war hero, Matt Rafferty. I'm so proud of you. But that's not a worry anymore. I've decided that I won't be holding office anywhere but Kerry Springs."

He frowned. "What about all your dreams about going to Washington?"

She shrugged. "I realized it was more my dad's dream."

"You're sure?"

She nodded. "There's so much to do right here in Kerry Springs. And after finding C.J., I know now I want to help other kids, too. Don't forget there are several empty structures downtown, one could easily be turned into a shelter, or a soup kitchen to help feed people."

He looked at her. "Could you use a partner?"

"What kind of partner?"

"A life partner." Matt surprised her when he walked to his horse, dug through the saddlebag and came back with a small velvet box. "Don't think I took anything for granted, but I wanted to be prepared in case I got lucky. Most importantly, I had to prove to you, I'm serious. To prove how much you mean to me." He released a breath. "I already have your brother's blessing, but it's important to me and to you to have your parents', too. We'll talk to them together. That is if you agree."

She couldn't believe this was happening. "Matt…"

He removed his hat as he went down on one knee. A soft breeze ruffled his dark hair. Here exposed to the elements on the land they both loved. It was a perfect setting. Yet, all Alisa could see was the handsome man she loved.

"Alisa, I've made a lot of mistakes over the years, but the second I fell in love with you, I knew I wanted to be the best man I could be for you. I'm still working on that. I want a future with you, to be your partner, your lover and husband. I love you. Alisa Merrick, will you marry me?"

"Yes. Oh, Matt. Yes!" Her hand shook as he slipped the ring on her finger. Then she pulled him to his feet and her mouth covered his. By the time he raised his head, they were both smiling and turned to watch the most perfect sunset.

Alisa eyed her beautiful pear-shaped diamond ring. He had wonderful taste. "You know this news will break a lot of women's hearts."

"Haven't I convinced you, you're the only woman I care about?"

She was still beaming. "Payback will be that we'll

probably have a houseful of daughters, and you'll have to protect them from every guy in town."

She glanced up to see him swallow. "How many is a houseful?"

"Depends on the size of the house."

He gave one of those sexy Rafferty grins. It melted her heart and did funny things to her stomach. She had no doubt it always would.

"Then I think we should get started on the family as soon as possible," he suggested.

Alisa countered, "I'll race you back to the house."

She started for her horse, and he reached for her. "There you go again, darlin', speeding around. Haven't you learned yet, that can get you into trouble?"

"That's exactly what I'm looking for, cowboy. Trouble. But only with you."

EPILOGUE

It was the end of the summer, and a wooden stage had been set up in the park. Red, white and blue balloons and paper streamers hung along the top of the temporary platform. The high school band was tuning up preparing to play for today's festivities.

Matt stood back under a large tree and watched his soon-to-be-bride, directing people to their jobs. He leaned against the tree trunk and thought back over the past six months, starting with the day Alisa had come back into his life.

He was lucky to have found her again. It had taken a while, but he was learning all about trust, too. They had been attending couple's counseling with the priest for their upcoming wedding. The big church affair was happening in mid-September. They both wanted to wait until the opening of the new Boys and Girls Club. It was the main focus for new council member Merrick and she had convinced the other members to support her ideas. Matt had a feeling it would be the first of many projects for this town. Over these past few months he'd been lucky to watch her work. To see her vision come to life.

Smiling, Matt stood. "You're looking mighty happy these days," a familiar voice said.

He turned to see his father. "I have a lot to be happy about."

Matt had spent a lot of time talking with his family, discussing the buried feelings they had for Patty Rafferty. It was helping to give them all some closure. And having Alisa's love and understanding helped, too.

Sean grinned. "I told you. It's all about finding that right woman."

He agreed. "I never thought I could feel this way. I'm one lucky guy."

"I think she got lucky with you, too. If I haven't told you lately, I've been proud of you, son, as I am of Evan. A father couldn't ask for any more than how well you both turned out."

So many things had changed for the better for the entire Rafferty family. Sean's Texas Barbecue Sauce was now on store shelves, giving Dad and Beth an added bonus to their retirement.

Rafferty's Legacy Vineyard was also doing well as was Evan's winery. He was able to buy out his silent partner, Alex Casali. Jenny was now doing weddings at the vineyard.

For him, Rafferty's Place was going great. Lori was his main waitress during their busy lunch hour. She'd had so many great ideas to help improve the restaurant, Matt couldn't keep up. Best part, he could leave her in charge if he wanted to steal Alisa away for some time together.

Kevin Ross had become more than a bartender, too. He learned fast and Matt had made him the night manager. They ended up becoming friends, too. It had been Kevin who convinced him to join a PTSD support group in San Antonio. The group met with other soldiers who'd served their country and needed help returning to society and their families.

That would be Alisa's and his next project. To use one of the meeting rooms at the Boys and Girls Club to start up a local group.

Alisa had several projects in mind. His top project was to get married to this wonderful woman.

His future bride wandered over to him. Smiling, he automatically opened his arms and wrapped her in a tight embrace.

She kissed him. "Hello, cowboy."

"Hello, Ms. Council Member. No doubt I'll be calling you mayor before long."

"You know that might just satisfy Dad. The family always thought that the Kerrys took too much credit. The town could have just as easily been called Merrickville."

Matt laughed. "Is that one of those crazy stories your dad told you?"

She grinned. "Maybe."

"I love you." He kissed the end of her nose. "You need any help with the ceremony?"

She shook her head. "It's under control. I just wanted to spend a little time with my-husband-to-be."

Alisa loved being in Matt's arms. She still had to pinch herself to believe they would soon be married.

She'd never been so happy. She glanced around the park. "Look, there's Evan and Jenny," she said and they both waved. Matt's sister-in-law was close to delivering another baby, a girl this time. They were talking to Sloan and Jade, doting over their baby boy, John Clayton Merrick. She looked over her shoulder at Matt. "Have you seen how much Johnny C has grown?"

"Yeah, as Dad would say, he's a strappin' lad." Matt

pressed his mouth against her ear. "I bet our babies will be prettier. And I have no problem letting Clay groom little Johnny to be the next Merrick senator."

Alisa grinned. They weren't going to wait too long before starting their family, and she was excited about that. "I can't wait until we're married."

"And we start making babies of our own."

She turned in his arms to face him. "We're going to be great parents. Look how well C.J. turned out."

He nodded, glad he and Lori had decided to make Kerry Springs their home. "I hope you don't mind if I spend time with him."

"Of course not. I love the boy, too. It's hard to believe just months ago we found him in the same building." She looked at the newly remodeled Boys and Girls Club.

She felt Matt's arms tighten around her middle. They were both remembering the bad times, but mostly all the good times that got them together.

Alisa knew she had to go back to work. She turned in Matt's arms as people began to gather around the bandstand. "After the celebration is over," she began, "we'll steal away and head back to the homestead house?"

"You gonna make it worth my while?" he teased.

"What do you think?" She wrapped her arms around his neck and rose up to meet him halfway as their lips touched in a sweet kiss that slowly turned hot. She broke it off.

"Slow down, cowboy. I think you're the one speeding now."

He grinned. "It's your fault." He kissed her nose. "You always distract me."

"Well, we can't get distracted until this party is over."

Matt laughed. "Who are you kidding, darlin'?" He

nodded toward the center of town. "This will never be over."

"So I care about my community."

"And I like that you care so much."

Alisa looked up and down Main Street. "Look, Matt. It's coming alive again." She glanced toward the Blind Stitch Quilt Shop. It was a meeting place for women to share their lives, their families. Shaffer's Ice Cream Parlor had had a facelift and now was a kids' hang-out. The same with the video arcade. It was no longer a place that had to be shut down for selling drugs, but had been purchased by Alex Casali and would soon be opened as a pizza place. Definitely for families. They were both a big part of revitalizing this town.

"We did good work." He pulled her close. "We make a good team, Alisa. You and I."

Alisa had dreamed about Matt Rafferty for so long and soon they'd be married. "Just keep saying it, so I believe it."

"How about if I show you?" He lowered his head and his mouth closed over hers in a hungry kiss. Soon the rest of the world disappeared. It was all about them being together. Forever.

Then the cheers started, and Alisa pulled back. She grinned with her future husband securely at her side. Together they were planting roots deep into their town, Kerry Springs. And for all the generations to come.

* * * * *

Mills & Boon® Hardback
March 2012

ROMANCE

Roccanti's Marriage Revenge	Lynne Graham
The Devil and Miss Jones	Kate Walker
Sheikh Without a Heart	Sandra Marton
Savas's Wildcat	Anne McAllister
The Argentinian's Solace	Susan Stephens
A Wicked Persuasion	Catherine George
Girl on a Diamond Pedestal	Maisey Yates
The Theotokis Inheritance	Susanne James
The Good, the Bad and the Wild	Heidi Rice
The Ex Who Hired Her	Kate Hardy
A Bride for the Island Prince	Rebecca Winters
Pregnant with the Prince's Child	Raye Morgan
The Nanny and the Boss's Twins	Barbara McMahon
Once a Cowboy...	Patricia Thayer
Mr Right at the Wrong Time	Nikki Logan
When Chocolate Is Not Enough...	Nina Harrington
Sydney Harbour Hospital: Luca's Bad Girl	Amy Andrews
Falling for the Sheikh She Shouldn't	Fiona McArthur

HISTORICAL

Untamed Rogue, Scandalous Mistress	Bronwyn Scott
Honourable Doctor, Improper Arrangement	Mary Nichols
The Earl Plays With Fire	Isabelle Goddard
His Border Bride	Blythe Gifford

MEDICAL

Dr Cinderella's Midnight Fling	Kate Hardy
Brought Together by Baby	Margaret McDonagh
The Firebrand Who Unlocked His Heart	Anne Fraser
One Month to Become a Mum	Louisa George

Mills & Boon® Large Print

March 2012

ROMANCE

The Power of Vasilii	Penny Jordan
The Real Rio D'Aquila	Sandra Marton
A Shameful Consequence	Carol Marinelli
A Dangerous Infatuation	Chantelle Shaw
How a Cowboy Stole Her Heart	Donna Alward
Tall, Dark, Texas Ranger	Patricia Thayer
The Boy is Back in Town	Nina Harrington
Just An Ordinary Girl?	Jackie Braun

HISTORICAL

The Lady Gambles	Carole Mortimer
Lady Rosabella's Ruse	Ann Lethbridge
The Viscount's Scandalous Return	Anne Ashley
The Viking's Touch	Joanna Fulford

MEDICAL

Cort Mason – Dr Delectable	Carol Marinelli
Survival Guide to Dating Your Boss	Fiona McArthur
Return of the Maverick	Sue MacKay
It Started with a Pregnancy	Scarlet Wilson
Italian Doctor, No Strings Attached	Kate Hardy
Miracle Times Two	Josie Metcalfe

Mills & Boon® *Hardback*

April 2012

ROMANCE

A Deal at the Altar	Lynne Graham
Return of the Moralis Wife	Jacqueline Baird
Gianni's Pride	Kim Lawrence
Undone by his Touch	Annie West
The Legend of de Marco	Abby Green
Stepping out of the Shadows	Robyn Donald
Deserving of his Diamonds?	Melanie Milburne
Girl Behind the Scandalous Reputation	Michelle Conder
Redemption of a Hollywood Starlet	Kimberly Lang
Cracking the Dating Code	Kelly Hunter
The Cattle King's Bride	Margaret Way
Inherited: Expectant Cinderella	Myrna Mackenzie
The Man Who Saw Her Beauty	Michelle Douglas
The Last Real Cowboy	Donna Alward
New York's Finest Rebel	Trish Wylie
The Fiancée Fiasco	Jackie Braun
Sydney Harbour Hospital: Tom's Redemption	Fiona Lowe
Summer With A French Surgeon	Margaret Barker

HISTORICAL

Dangerous Lord, Innocent Governess	Christine Merrill
Captured for the Captain's Pleasure	Ann Lethbridge
Brushed by Scandal	Gail Whitiker
Lord Libertine	Gail Ranstrom

MEDICAL

Georgie's Big Greek Wedding?	Emily Forbes
The Nurse's Not-So-Secret Scandal	Wendy S. Marcus
Dr Right All Along	Joanna Neil
Doctor on Her Doorstep	Annie Claydon

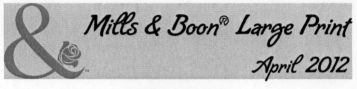
Mills & Boon® Large Print

April 2012

ROMANCE

Jewel in His Crown	Lynne Graham
The Man Every Woman Wants	Miranda Lee
Once a Ferrara Wife...	Sarah Morgan
Not Fit for a King?	Jane Porter
Snowbound with Her Hero	Rebecca Winters
Flirting with Italian	Liz Fielding
Firefighter Under the Mistletoe	Melissa McClone
The Tycoon Who Healed Her Heart	Melissa James

HISTORICAL

The Lady Forfeits	Carole Mortimer
Valiant Soldier, Beautiful Enemy	Diane Gaston
Winning the War Hero's Heart	Mary Nichols
Hostage Bride	Anne Herries

MEDICAL

Breaking Her No-Dates Rule	Emily Forbes
Waking Up With Dr Off-Limits	Amy Andrews
Tempted by Dr Daisy	Caroline Anderson
The Fiancée He Can't Forget	Caroline Anderson
A Cotswold Christmas Bride	Joanna Neil
All She Wants For Christmas	Annie Claydon

#12 GEN STD LP